AXHOLME

Mike Bradwell was born in Scunthorpe, Lincolnshire, in 1948. He trained as an actor at East 15 and subsequently worked with Mike Leigh and the Ken Campbell Road Show. In 1971 he founded Hull Truck Theatre and ran it for eleven years. From 1996 to 2007 he was Artistic Director of the Bush Theatre, London, where he directed more than forty productions. He wrote and directed for many other theatre companies in the UK and abroad, and for film, television and radio. He died in April 2025.

Also by Mike Bradwell

The Reluctant Escapologist:
Adventures in Alternative Theatre

Inventing the Truth:
Devising and Directing for the Theatre

A Bed of Roses

MIKE BRADWELL

Axholme

CB editions

First published in the UK in 2026
by CB editions
146 Percy Road London W12 9QL
www.cbeditions.com

Printed in England by Short Run Press

ISBN 978-1-7394212-0-5

FOREWORD

Jim Broadbent

I met Mike Bradwell in 1976 in Amsterdam where we were both involved with separate productions at the Mickery Theatre. Curiously, given we knew we both came from Lincolnshire, it was not something we ever really discussed even though we became quite close over the next fifty years.

Lincolnshire is England's second largest county, second only to its neighbour Yorkshire, yet it is little known. It has a long flat North Sea coastline, a once thriving fishing industry in Grimsby, a once thriving steel industry in Scunthorpe, and an awful lot of agriculture. In the north-west corner, cut off from the rest of the county by the River Trent, is the little-known Isle of Axholme. It is not actually an island, but historically a wetland where areas of higher ground were settled, most notably the town of Epworth, the home of John Wesley, the founder of Methodism. Mike's book brings to vivid life what it was to grow up in this rural community in the 1950s, capturing in myriad ways the fun and games, the characters, the dramas and the tragedies, and all told in the unique Lincolnshire vernacular of a young lad and seen through his eyes.

I worked with Mike five times over the years, sharing enthusiasms and jokes, and though this book is not strictly autobiographical, I learnt so much about him through this window to a time and a place so remote from the metropolis we both found ourselves in, and it felt that somehow we were having conversations we had never had in person.

Coming from my own equally little-known corner of the county, I am able to vouch for the authenticity of his glorious vision of Axholme and to celebrate both it and him.

Axholme

The Swan's Nest

It was the day that Brent Robinson shat his sen that we went to see the swan's nest. Brent was three. Brent was Brian and Gordon's brother. Brian was an awkward little sod and Gordon was Ginger. When we first noticed that Brent had shat his sen everyone said bugger including Old Ma Bowers. That was swearing but it wasn't a Queen's word. A Queen's word was so bad that that you went to prison. Mr Robinson who was Brian, Ginger and Brent Robinsons dad had been to prison but not about saying a Queen's word. They had to bring Brent because Mr Robinson was driving a lorry on probation and Mrs Robinson was badly. Mr Robinson was called Ron but he called himself Tex. Ron Tex.

Old Ma Bowers had thought up the journey to see the swan's nest which was at Double Rivers along the road to

Scunny. Old Ma Bowers looked like a wheelbarrow. Paul Bowers was her grandson and he was a dwarf. Paul was the Professor aged eleven who had the whole village in a flutter. He was a juvenile lepidopterist and he had caught a Death's Head Hawk Moth that really Audrey Glew had found on a pile of seed potatoes in Barry Dodds's field next to the Drain. It was in the Epworth Bells. Old Ma Bowers pushed Paul in an old kids tin trolley. It was called a Triang Battlewagon. Paul looked like a wheelbarrow.

Coming too on the journey to look at the swan's nest were Roy Booth who went fishing and had some fantail pigeons and a love of nature and birdwatching and sometimes caught a monster roach and John Took who had a 22 air rifle and a greyhound called Mick that had a big scar on the back from barbed wire when they were hunting a partridge. Roy Booth lived on one side of the Drain and John Took lived on the other side down Green Lane. Kenny Blanchard couldn't go as he had to get his dads tea and Angela Whiteley came too because everyone had looked at her bottom and she lived next to Roy Booth.

The Drain was called the Folly Drain built by the Dutchman Cornelius Vermuyden to stop the village being a swamp. It used to have eels and Roy's dad used to skin them and eat them. But they went years ago when they had the pipe put in for the inside toilets. It still had tadpoles, and sticklebacks and frogs and water hens and ducks but it also had rats and the pipe smelled of polio. John Took hunted the rats and the ducks. There was a very old bridge over the Drain next to the old windmill. The last of the sails had been blown off the windmill in the big storm. They flew through the air and smashed in the lane. Someone could have been killed. Everybody went to the bridge after tea. There was also a lamp post and when the sun went down moths flew round the light and Paul Bowers and Old Ma Bowers tried to catch them in a net on the end of a brush. This was where Angela showed her bottom. Under the bridge.

Everyone met up at the bridge on the morning of the journey to see the swan's nest. The swan's nest was on one of the Double Rivers. Roy's dad Mr Booth had spotted it when coming back on his Norton from his night shift at the App Frod Steelworks in Scunny. He had told Old Ma Bowers because it was a rarity. Old Ma Bowers said all the swans belonged to the Queen and could break a man's leg with one blow of his wing. Everyone had brought sandwiches and pop and other stuff as well to have a picnic. Old Ma Bowers brought a flask of Camp coffee. Everyone had brought weapons just in case. Brian Robinson had a catapult. Ginger had a water pistol. Brent had a coat hanger. Paul Bowers had a butterfly net and a killing jar with embrocation in it to kill the butterflies in.

John Took took his 22 air rifle. He wasn't supposed to bring Mick the greyhound as he might try to hunt the swan that belonged to the Queen but Mick followed him anyway by swimming over the Drain even when John chucked stones at him. Roy had his binocs to see birds.

Angela Whiteley had a big round face with nowt in it. So we set off with the Battlewagon.

It was at the back of the beyond. To get there we had to cross the Big Turbary and to get to the Big Turbary we had to walk along the path on the bank of the Drain past Roy's house and pigeon loft. There were loads of other birds to watch. There were hedge sparrows and thrushes and blackbirds and greenfinches and reed warblers and a chaffinch and wood pigeons and rooks and magpies. The butterflies were meadow browns, peacocks, red admirals, coppers, small blues, large whites and a six spot burnet. Roy said he saw a sparrow hawk but he didn't. Half way along the lane was the madwoman's house. It was covered in creepers and brambles and all the gates had rusty padlocks and the windows were blocked up but some had curtains like cobwebs. Jackdaws nested in the ivy. Like a witches house if there were any. The madwoman had gone mad when she lost her husband or summat ages ago and Old Ma Bowers said there was a story there. They kept her in the attic. She got out once and went to the village howling like a dog. Jim Heals the joiner who was creosoting a shed saw her and shouted that the madwoman was out and then everyone shouted out that the madwoman was out and people went and hid under the table and drew their curtains like when it was the King's funeral. People were terrified because she might have had an axe but the madwoman didn't get anybody and they caught her and put her in a loony bin in Donny and gave her electricity. But she came back and was locked in the attic again by her brother who lived in the house and guarded her. Everyone kept dead quiet when we passed the loony madwoman witches house. Mick the greyhound got into the yard and chased the chickens but no one came out. The madwoman's brother sold eggs and other local produce on Epworth market.

On the way down the lane Old Ma Bowers sang a song about going a wandering along the mountain track with a nap sack on her back and singing Valerie. Gordon Robinson made up a poem about Rabbit the Bunny going to Scunny without any money which was funny.

At the bottom of the lane was a five bar gate that led to the Big Turbary. The gate was to stop cows and sheep getting out. The Turbary in olden days was a Common where the common people could get turf from the bogs to burn on their fires before coal. Also you could graze your sheep and cows if you had any and it was free. Nowadays it was just a really big field with ponds and swamps that Vermuyden didn't drain. There were loads of water hens and partridges and dragon flies and bullrushes. There were hundreds of gorse bushes full of linnets and yellow hammers. There were skylarks in the sky and peewits. On one side was the Drain and on the other the old Sandtoft aerodrome where they used to have Itie prisoners of war. And there was the wing of a crashed Lancashire bomber that some pigs ate out of. A muddy track ran all the way across the Turbary. The mud was chewed up by Howard Kirk's Massey Ferguson tractor. Howard Kirk was an

Agricultural Merchant who sold peas, washed carrots and potatoes. He lived in Common Farm on the far side of the Turbary. It did not belong to common people now, It belonged to Howard Kirk who was a self made man. Some of the Big Turbary was now black and dead. It was poisoned by some drums of poisonous weed killer dumped there. Old Ma Bowers said Jim Heals had told her that Howard Kirk had dumped the weed killer. A cow had been poisoned but it wasn't Howard Kirk's.

The five bar gate was locked because of the poisoned cow. There was sign saying Keep Out. Someone had shot it to pieces with a 12 bore. Brian Robinson shot it with his catty. Ginger shot it with his water pistol. John Took shot it with his airgun. Old Ma Bowers said it was illegal and also bloody hell because they had to lift the Battlewagon over the gate and Paul. Brian and Gordon had to lift Brent over the gate who said he was badly and wanted to go home. Mick the greyhound found a way through the fence and ran off after rabbits. The muddy track was very muddy. We should have brought wellies.

The Triang Battlewagon wouldn't go down the muddy track so we had to keep to the side in the nettles then Freddie Swash drove Howard Kirk's Massey Ferguson Tractor dead fast down the lane and splashed up the mud so it went all over Brian Robinson. He did it on purpose. He didn't like Brian or Ron Tex.

They didn't like him. Freddie Swash was Howard Kirk's foreman. Brian shot at him with his catty. Freddie told him to Queen's word off and tried to run him over. Then there was a cuckoo but we never saw it. Then after a bit we found a grassy bumpy bit near a pond with dragon flies and we got out our picnic and the sun came out. We put it all out on Angela's raincoat. The sandwiches were potted meat and Kraft cheese slices. There were some hard boiled eggs and Penguins and Dandelion and Burdock. You could get money back on the bottles. Paul Bowers caught a small tortoise butterfly in his net and put it in his killing jar where it fluttered to death. There was suddenly a rotten smell. Brent had shat his sen.

Brent's shit ran down the leg of his shorts and on to his shoes and everyone said bugger including Old Ma Bowers. Brent started crying as Old Ma Bowers pulled off his pants and wiped his bottom with dock leaves. Everyone nearly puked up. Old Ma Bowers washed Brent's shitty pants in the pond. She was going to put them on a gorse bush to dry but we hadn't got the time and Gordon Robinson said his mam would kill him if Brent went home without pants. So Old Ma Bowers lifted up her skirt and took off her own knickers and put them on Brent. Nobody wanted to carry Brent's wet pants home so Old Ma Bowers put them in Angela's nap sack. Old Ma Bowers was good for her age. She had won half a crown kicking a penalty past Donny Rovers reserve goalkeeper Billy Brough at the Armthorpe Miners Welfare Gala. Rovers first team goalkeeper was Harry Gregg, soon to be the hero of Munich.

When Brent had shut up about wearing Old Ma

Bowers big pants we set off to the far end of the Big Turbary. Nothing much happened until we got the far end where there was a padlocked old gate that nobody ever used except Howard Kirk for his tractor. People had carved old names on it. It wasn't even Howard Kirk's gate but Brian and Gordon and John Took took it off its hinges and threw it in the ditch like Mischief Night. Old Ma Bowers said serves him right and it would save us having to get the Battlewagon and Professor Paul and Brent over the gate. The reason Paul Bowers was a dwarf was because he had polio.

After the gate was a gravel track that you could go down three ways. One went up to the main road at the top to the village. One went down to the Engine Drain. The middle one went past Common Farm up to the thin wood near the road to Keadby Bridge near Double Rivers where the swan's nest was. We went down the middle one. Howard Kirk had lots of fields everywhere and some of them were around Common Farm where he lived. One field used to have pigs on it but now it had Gillian Kirk's pony Stargazer that cost thousands of pounds. They were teaching it to jump fences so Jim Heals built some out of planks of wood and fertiliser drums. Some had dead branches nailed on to make them look like a hedge. One was painted red, white and blue. There were a few pullets and a guinea fowl and an old green railway carriage where the special rabbits had been. It had a wire fence all round it so Stargazer couldn't jump out. Gillian Kirk was the apple of Howard Kirk's eye. She had a brother called Raymond who was fat and had titties. They went to posh schools in Donny where you had to pay so Howard Kirk had to make sacrifices.

Before you got to the farmhouse there was a giant barn made out of corrugated iron. Inside was the carrot washing machine. There were huge hose pipes for the carrot washing water and another hose pipe to take it away to water the field at the back. There were hundreds of house sparrows called spuggies and swallows nesting in the barn and the barn smelled of bird shit. John Took shot loads of spuggies. Howard Kirk would be happy. The feathers from the nests and the shit clogged up his carrot washer. The field at the back was where Howard Kirk grew his peas. Every year most of the wives in the village and some lasses and some gypos and squatters went to pick the peas and Old Ma Bowers, Paul and Angela Whiteley and Mrs Ada Robinson and Brent and Mrs Glew and Audrey. Everybody met up on the bridge and got in the back of Howard Kirk's old RAF ambulance which he got at the auction when they sold up Sandtoft aerodrome after the Ities were let out. Freddie Swash was driving and too fast. When you got to the pea field you got a big sack and went off and picked the peas. It took hours to fill a sack. Then you took it to Freddie Swash who weighed it on a weighing machine and if there were enough peas he gave you a bus ticket with three and six written on it and then you picked some more peas. Some of the wives had some beer. When it got to teatime Howard Kirk and fat Raymond turned up in his bronze 3.4 litre Mark VII Jaguar and it was time to get your money. Everyone queued up by the car door. Howard Kirk sat in the driving seat smoking a fat cigar. Fat Raymond sat in the passenger seat and handed out the wages. You gave him your three and six bus ticket and he gave you the money out of a big doctor's bag. Some women had loads of bus tickets. Then Howard Kirk drove off in the bronze Jaguar Mark VII. He had done alright for his sen. He had already sold all his peas to the canning factory in Selby. Everyone got back in the RAF ambulance and Freddie drove like a maniac. Back at the bridge everyone went home for tea but Old Ma Bowers and some others went to The Wheatsheaf because it was back breaking work. Uncle Walter was the landlord of The Wheatsheaf.

After Common Farm was another field. It might have been potatoes. This field was just ploughed black earth with muck spread all over it. This was manure. It stank like stink bombs. There was a huge electric pylon for the electric for Common Farm which made a zizzing noise and birds didn't perch on it or they would have died of shock. Then there was a long hawthorn hedge which had loads of cuddies and some yellow hammers. Behind the hawthorn hedge was the old swimming pool which had gone mouldy and was full of old tyres and rotten pea sacks etc. The thin wood was where Roy Booth's dad caught the snake. Mr Booth had been fishing for monster pike in the Double Rivers. He went into the wood and saw the snake on a tree stump. He threw his coat over it and put it in his bait tin to take back to Roy. Roy had a tin bath of water where he kept all sorts of animals etc. When there was tadpoles he had tadpoles and frogs and toads. He had some slugs and larvae and weeds. All from the Drain. It had a plastic lid with holes in it for a roof. Everybody came to see Roy's snake. It was supposed to be a grass snake. Old Ma Bowers said it was an adder and it was poisonous and it could kill you. So they looked it up in the Observers Book of British Wildlife and it was an adder but it didn't matter because it got out of the bath and Ron Tex Robinson ran over it with his lorry.

They were going to feed it to the cats but thought they might get poisoned so Mrs Robinson put it round Brian's cowboy hat with some glue but it just went rotten and he threw it in the Drain.

The thin wood was thin but it had hundreds of tall trees. Some of them were a Rookery. This was hundreds of rook's nests made of big sticks with thousands of rooks. Rooks have a white bump on their beaks. Crows don't. The cawing was very loud. When they flew up it was like night. John Took wanted to get their eggs, Roy Booth said leave them alone. The tree was very tall and it was dangerous but John Took could climb like a monkey and Brian gave him a leg up. John went up the tree like a monkey. Brian started to climb up behind him but a branch broke and Brian had to come back down. Angela screamed.

Old Ma Bowers told John Took to come down but he didn't. When John got to the nests the rooks went barmy and tried to peck his eyes out. Mick barked like mad and the rooks all squawked like mad and the sky went like night. John took loads of eggs from loads of nests and put them in his pockets and in his cap to get them down. He put some in his gob. Rook's eggs are bluish green to greyish green with heavy ash grey and brown blotching. When John climbed down the rooks went mad again. He had to jump from where the branch had broken.

When he hit the ground the eggs in his gob broke and John puked them out all over the grass. The eggs were bubbed and the slimy bloody half rook chicks lay in a pool of yellow stuff that looked like snot. Then there was a fight.

Roy said the John was a murderer for taking the bubbed eggs and shooting all the spuggies. John told him to Queen's word off. Roy hit John with his binoculars so John pushed him to the ground and got on top and punched him but Roy got his legs round John's neck in a scissors hold like Masambula the undefeated African witchdoctor on the wrestling in Bridlington and squeezed so John couldn't breathe. But he couldn't hold it and John grabbed his hair and got him in a Chinese death grip and said submit and Mick the greyhound was going to bite Roy so Roy submitted. And cried. There was also a wrestler called Billy Two-Rivers and we were at a place called Double Rivers. Billy Two-Rivers was a red Indian. Old Ma Bowers said that it was alright to take bird's eggs if you left a few. Gordon Robinson had been on a class trip to Donny museum and they had hundreds there in glass cases. They had ostriches and eagle's eggs. So John Took shared out the rest of the rook's eggs and everybody got one except Roy.

A swan's nest is made out of loads of sticks and weeds. It's like a big rook's nest but on a river. When we got to the Double Rivers river we couldn't see the swan's nest. There was a swan that flew away hissing down the river as soon as it saw us and Mick the greyhound and the Battlewagon. We looked along the river bank for the swan's nest and Roy found it through his binocs.

Everybody except John looked at it through Roy's binocs which cheered Roy up. The nest was empty. There was nowt in it. No swans, no eggs, no cygnets. No nowt. It looked smashed up. There were a few feathers and some on the river bank. Maybe rats had got it. Or kids. Gordon got a big swan feather and put it on his head like a red Indian. Like Billy Two-Rivers. Like Tonto.

We went home the other way along the Engine Drain past the old Sandtoft aerodrome where there were hundreds of peewits. John Took went home back past Common Farm on his own because he was fed up. Brent couldn't walk anymore so Brian gave him a piggy back. The reason we had gone the other way was because when you got to the Engine Drain there was a pub called the Bridge Inn and Old Ma Bowers had some Double Diamond works wonders and we had pop and crisps. When we got back to our bridge over the Drain it was getting dark and the midges were about. Brian and Ginger had taken Brent home still in Old Ma Bowers big knickers. Old Ma Bowers pulled Paul home in the Battlewagon. Paul had not got polio from the Drain but from somewhere else.

Roy and Angela were standing on the bridge when they saw John Took and Mick a long way off on John's side of the Dyke. They were ratting. Roy and Angela shouted murderer. John gave them a V sign. They shouted murderer again. John shot at them with the airgun. It was a really long way away and a fluke. There was a whistle and the pellet hit Angela in the face. She fell over like she had been shot. It wasn't too bad. There was no blood. It wasn't as bad as a wasp sting. Angela had a mark and a bruise for a week. But it could have taken her eye out. She daren't tell her mam cos John would have split on her being rude with everybody seeing her bottom. After John Took shot Angela in the face nobody talked to him for a bit but then everybody got over it.

The Threshing Machine

On the morning before the mice there was a big old steam traction engine parked in Ron Tex Robinson's yard where he kept his lorry and other goods. It was hundreds of years old and weighed tons and had big iron wheels and you needed a ladder to get up to the driver's seat. It was rusty and brown and had old paint falling off and you could see the old green painted letters Fountain's Fairground Attractions. It was black with soot and smelled of diesel oil. It had an old rusty boiler that used to burn the coal that boiled the water that made the steam and a tall black chimney. These days it ran on diesel oil. It had a big steam whistle. We all climbed over it until the man who worked the boiler gave Brian Robinson a clip round the ear. It was here to work the threshing machine that was already in Barry Dodds's field next to the Drain. Barry Dodds owned the garage next to the field and mended tractors and seed riddles and cultivators. He got the garage and the field when Old Man Dodds fell down the inspection pit and broke his neck. Barry wasn't that old when this happened. He got the garage which was called Selwyn Motors and the field and a breakdown lorry and rented the field out to Howard Kirk. Howard Kirk used the field for his haystacks which were mountains of straw as big as the Methodist Chapel. They were there to dry out before threshing. They were covered in big tarpaulins held down by ropes tied to rocks and old metal bars to keep out the rain. People got under the tarpaulins and made dens and did other things. There were two haystacks in the field. The reason that they were in Barry's field was because you could get the water from the Drain for the steam for the steam engine for the threshing machine.

The threshing machine was a huge machine that threshed wheat. It was made out of wood and iron bars and chains and it cut and smashed and crushed the wheat that came from the haystacks with big blades and spikes. It was painted red and there was a big sign saying Marshalls of Gainsborough which was where it came from. It looked like a crazy fun fair machine. There were flying wheels that went round really fast and leather driving belts and it was too dangerous to get near to it. People had their skin flayed off and a woman from near Haxey had her arm pulled out of its socket. You stood on top of the haystack with pitchforks and forked the wheat stooks into the threshing machine and they came out as chaff and straw and the grain came out the other end and went into sacks. Then Howard Kirk sold the sacks. It made a noise like the Cake Walk at Wonderland at Cleethorpes but lots louder. Freddie Swash and Howard Kirk's farm men mostly did the forking but people in the village joined in and got paid. Ron Tex Robinson and Jim Heals always came and Uncle Walter who ran The Wheatsheaf. Even Howard Kirk in his jag smoking his fat cigar got his sen over to help and fat Raymond. There were some dogs and Mick the greyhound.

Next morning at about six o'clock they fired up the traction engine and blew the steam whistle and thick black oily smoke came out of the chimney as it rolled into Dodds's field. Freddie Swash and Barry put down wooden planks to stop it sinking into the grass. They rigged up the steam engine to the threshing machine and set it going. It sounded like an earthquake going off. All the chickens and Roy Booth's fantails and the water hens on the Drain and the dogs all went mad. Everybody got given jobs, pitch forking etc. John Took got told to do filling grain bags and fat Raymond had to turn a wheel but he got it stuck so Roy Booth took over. Everybody else got ready for the mice including Paul Bowers who had new leg irons for the polio and crutches.

There were thousands of mice living in the haystacks. When the stacks were pulled apart and thrown into the threshing machine the mice ran out. Everybody was waiting with big sticks with nails in them and iron bars even Paul Bowers. They clubbed the mice and smashed their heads in. There was loads of blood and the mice ran about squealing. John Took shot some with the 22 airgun and they exploded. It was alright though because mice are vermin.

The steam engine made the air boiling hot. The chaff was blowing around like in a sand storm. You couldn't breathe so everybody put hankies over their mouth, or scarfs. Everybody looked like bandits or outlaws or cattle rustlers. Like in The Lone Ranger we were the baddies.

The threshing was back breaking work and mouse hunting and everyone had a break for dinner. Mrs Booth and Angela's mam and Mrs Glew brought loads of stuff and plates and knives and forks and cups. They had potted meat and Kraft sliced cheese sandwiches and hard boiled eggs. Old Ma Bowers had made a meat and potato pie in a bucket. Howard Kirk got a crate of hot beer out of the boot of the bronze Mark VII jaguar for the men. The third Mrs Kirk and Gillian came in the third Mrs Kirk's blue Austin A30. Gillian had her arm in a sling because Stargazer had thrown her off. They had made some tinned salmon sandwiches and a chocolate cake. We had some Dandelion and Burdock from Fletchers shop which was at the end of the lane that went down to Dodds's garage. You could get money back on the bottles. After the meat and potato pie was over Ginger Gordon got the bucket and washed it out in the Dyke. When the men had a nap or went to Barry Dodds's toilet Brian and Roy and Paul and John Took and Brent who was there now and Angela Whiteley and fat Raymond got all the dead mice and put them in the bucket. Some of them were only nearly dead. Then we hung the bucket up on a fence so Mick and other dogs couldn't get at it. Then the steam whistle blew and the earthquake thresher started up again. And we went back to work. The men were very sweaty and sang a song about inky pinky parly voo.

There were less mice after dinner. Then Mrs Kirk took Gillian and Raymond home to Common Farm in the Austin A30. Raymond got the munk on because he wanted to stay and do the mice but Mrs Kirk said it was common and germs and made him get into the car and he did. The third Mrs Kirk was called Olive Oil and she was the third because the other two were dead. It had been a mistake because she was years younger than him and he had been born in 1898. She was not from around here. Olive Oil had met Howard Kirk and his second wife Grace in Bridlington where she went to get better from smallpox that she had caught when she was a nurse looking after people with smallpox.

The second Mrs Kirk Grace was there in Brid with her daughter Fran and Mr Kirk. They gave Olive Oil a job to come and look after Fran because she was a handful. And it was alright for ages and Olive Oil and Grace also bred the special rabbits in an old railway carriage and then

Grace got sick and Olive had to look after her too until Grace died and Fran went nursing in Kettering. Olive Oil was scared of what the neighbours will say as there was just her and Howard Kirk left at Common Farm and she had nowhere else to go anyway and he had loads of money. So she married Howard Kirk who was pleased about it. Old Ma Bowers knew all about it and that summat was up as Olive Oil was always miserable and God knows how they came to have kids because she never wanted any. Nobody ever said owt about the first Mrs Kirk.

The reason Stargazer had thrown off Gillian was because when she was getting on fat Raymond had hit him on the bum with a riding crop. Stargazer had kicked out and stood up on his back legs and Gillian fell off and got knocked out. Raymond thought she was dead and shouted out Stargazer has killed Gillian and said it was nowt to do with him but they took her to Scunthorpe General Hospital and she only had a sprained wrist. Stargazer bolted and they sent out a search party to find him but he had disappeared into thin air. Everyone in the village looked everywhere because there was going be a reward as Stargazer was worth thousands of pounds. All the farm men looked as well and fat Raymond. Then Angela Whiteley found him a long way off. He had gone down the lane past the snake wood and the aerodrome and along the bank of the Engine Drain to miles past the Bridge Inn. He was eating a pile of thistles.

Angela walked straight up to him and got hold of his

bridle. He let her lead him back through the village all along Westgate all on her own. People came out to look. When they got to our bridge Howard Kirk was waiting with a horsebox.

Everyone clapped Angela and patted Stargazer and gave him carrots and sugar lumps except John Took who shouted out show us your bottom. Howard Kirk shook Angela's hand and gave her a ten bob note.

At the end of the day they had threshed the first haystack and Howard Kirk gave Jim Heals and Mr Booth and Barry Dodds etc some wages for the days work and everybody else got a shilling. Then all the men went to The Wheatsheaf and Howard bought some rounds. Freddie Swash and Jim Heals had to guard the threshing machine all night in case any other farmers tried to steal it. Ginger Robinson went to Fletchers and got the money back on the Dandelion and Burdock and got some brown paper bags like they put apples in. When Ginger got back with the bags Brian got the mouse bucket off the fence and we sorted out the mice six in each bag and Roy Booth got a wheelbarrow from Jim Heals woodyard and we went off to sell them but not Paul Bowers who couldn't walk yet much even with his new polio leg irons and crutches and Brent who had caught a mouse in a jam jar and had taken it home for his mam.

Everybody shouted dead mice for sale dead mice for your cat give your moggie a treat a tanner a bag. And stuff like that. We went all along Westgate and up Green Lane and then Carr House Lane. All the women bought some mice and some a few bags to put in the fridge. Everybody said it was a bargain. We went as far as the Little Turbary which was the other way from the Big Turbary and Kenny Blanchard sold some to the woman with all the pigs who didn't even have cats so maybe fed them to the pigs. When we got back to our bridge it was dark and everyone was covered in dried blood and mouse bits.

There was loads of money. Roy Booth counted it and shared it all out. He shared out a bob for Paul and a tanner for Brent who weren't there. John Took said Angela shouldn't have any as she had got the reward for finding Stargazer. Gordon Robinson said that we could sell other stuff like washed carrots and we could get some off of fat Raymond.

Nothing much happened on the next day with the threshing machine and the second haystack as the mice had gone except John Took got caught short and went for a shit behind a bush and Angela Whiteley picked up his airgun and shot him up the bum.

The Swimming Pool

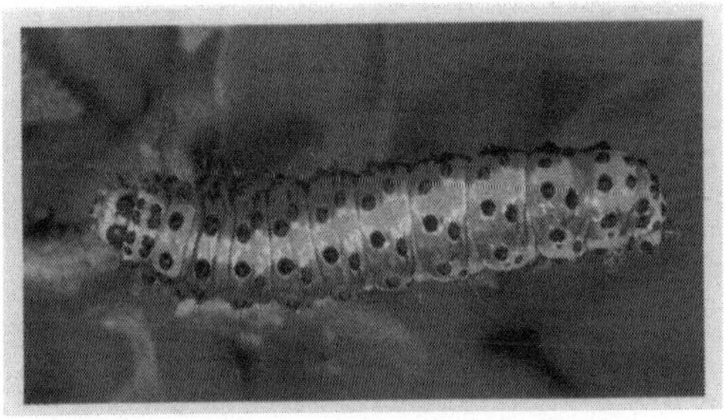

Fat Raymond Kirk and Gillian went to posh schools in Donny which was a sacrifice. Olive Oil took them there every day in her blue Austin A30. It was fifteen mile each way. It was worth it because they wouldn't turn out common like the Robinsons and then they could go to school up London. Gillian went to a school for girls and Raymond went to the Mount school which was near the Race Course where they had the Saint Ledger. To get to Donny you had to go across the old Sandtoft aerodrome even when it was icy in winter and when the yellow smog came down. Olive Oil was miserable and told Raymond every day that she wished he had never been born and she would swing for him. He was the runt of the litter. We knew this because Roy Booth's old sister Joyce once had to look after Raymond and Gillian and do some washing and cleaning. On Saturdays Howard Kirk took Raymond and Gillian to Donny when he was going to the market and the Wellington Inn with some other farmers. Gillian was going to Dora Cowley's ballet dancing class and Raymond went to Donny Rovers at the famous Bellevue ground with Fishy Addock who lived in Armthorpe where they had the pit.

This didn't happen now. This happened ages before now. Howard Kirk and Olive Oil and Raymond and Gillian went on holiday to abroad Majorca in a hotel. They went to a bullfight like Tommy Steele in Little White Bull and they all got the shits from the disgusting foreign food. The hotel that was loads cheaper than here had a swimming pool. Fat Raymond and Gillian went in it a lot and their skin peeled off. Howard and Olive Oil didn't go into the pool and drank some special sherry. They couldn't drink the disgusting foreign water because it was poison. When they got back Gillian Kirk was the apple of Howard's eye and wanted a swimming pool. This was before she wanted a pony. Last time it was hot Ron Tex Robinson had made a swimming pool in his yard out of cutting a big tyre from a Lancashire bomber in half and filling it with buckets from Whiteley's outside tap without telling him. It was good. We were all pirates with a skull and crossbones. This is not what Howard Kirk did.

Nobody round here had ever made a swimming pool before so Howard went to a mason builder in Goole he knew from The Wellington who built sheep dips which are like a swimming pool for disinfecting sheep with mange etc. Freddie Swash started by digging a big square hole with the Massey Ferguson tractor with the big hydraulic digging shovel on the front that they used for muck shifting. They put the hole in the back field on the other side of the hawthorn hedge so it would keep the wind off. In the hole they found some cat and dog skeletons and some old marbles and loads of rocks but no treasure. Then they put down some chicken wire and the Goole man came with a cement mixer and poured in a load of concrete. They made a hole for the water to run out into the ground. They propped up the concrete with planks and waited for it to dry.

When it was dry it looked like a big concrete hole. Then Jim Heals painted it with three coats of waterproof distemper. He told Old Ma Bowers that it was daft. It took two days to fill it up with the big hose with water from the carrot washer. It had to be ready for the party that Raymond and Gillian were having on Saturday so Howard Kirk could show off his money.

It was dead hot when Freddie Swash went to pick up all fat Raymond and Gillian's posh friends from their posh schools in Donny. Because it was hot they took one of Howard Kirk's open back Foden lorries he used for his agricultural products of peas, washed carrots and potatoes and tied on loads of balloons and Christmas tree decorations. Freddie picked them all up in The Wellington yard and they all kissed mummy and daddy goodbye. They all had posh clothes on. When they got to Hatfield straight Freddie Swash drove at about a hundred miles an hour and when he went over the bumps on the Hatfield level crossing they all screamed like on the big dipper at Cleethorpes. Only really. When the party lorry came through the village everybody shouted snobs etc and some threw stones and Ginger showed them his ginger ring.

At Common Farm they all got changed in the rabbit carriage and jumped into the water and had water fights and ducked the lasses and threw rubber tyre tubes at Raymond. They were out of control. Some farm dogs jumped in too. The night before there was a big wind and the hawthorn leaves had blown off the hawthorn hedge and into Howard's pool. Also loads of black and yellow hairy caterpillars who had drowned and gone slimy. Howard Kirk had fished some of them out with a landing net but there were loads left and germs and the water was scummy and you wouldn't want to drink it. Then they got out and had fights flicking towels. Then they all had tea on the grass where Howard Kirk grew his roses and Howard Kirk smoked a cigar. They had paper hats and tinned salmon and salad cream sandwiches and cucumbers and chocolate eclairs and cream horns and orangina. Then they had ice cream and jelly and had an ice cream and jelly fight which was bedlam. Then they had some games like pass the parcel and hide and seek in all the farm buildings and the muck shed and got their posh clothes filthy. Fat Raymond did not win any of the games even lucky dip when everyone got a prize. Then they all went home in the lorry and Freddie drove like a maniac and some were sick. When they all went home Gillian and fat Raymond sat on the grass by the roses and were mardy. They were spoilt brats.

We know all this because Old Ma Bowers and Roy Booth's big sister Joyce went to be servants. Old Ma Bowers took Paul with her and this was before he had the polio. They had to clean up all the mess from the party which was just disgusting and you would think a bomb had dropped. It was very hot so Paul and Old Ma Bowers and Joyce had a swim in the caterpillar swimming pool in their undies when no one was looking. Howard Kirk had gone to a meeting with some other farmers and masons and Olive Oil was having to lie down. It wasn't deep enough to swim in. Only three feet. But they splashed about.

When Raymond and Gillian got to school on Monday some posh kids were covered in spots and boils from the swimming pool and some were at home with sore throats etc. The posh kids mams were mad about the dead catcrpillar germs and shouted at Olive Oil. Mr Hay the headmaster of the Mount school phoned up Howard Kirk who told him it was nowt to do with him and he should mind his own business and he was paying through the nose anyway.

Some big boys beat up fat Raymond and pulled his titties. They didn't go to school for a bit. Ron Tex sold the Lancashire bomber tyres to the pig woman on the Little Turbary for five bob for pig troughs.

Polio

Paul Bowers didn't have polio straight away when he was born. He got it after the rotten caterpillars in Howard Kirk's swimming pool but they said he didn't. They said it was an outbreak. Old Ma Bowers looked after Paul. She was his nan and he lived in her old house which was up past Jim Heals woodyard and the butchers and Andersons shop. Paul's mam had run off with a sambo from RAF Finningley when Paul was five. Old Mr Bowers was also dead. He used to dig peoples gardens like Howard Kirk but had to stop with his chest and then he died. They had a big orchard but it was full of weeds and nettles and brambles. When Paul got polio he had to go to hospital because his spine stopped working and he couldn't breathe. They covered him in some plasticene then they put him in an iron lung which was a tube that pushed air in his lungs and he was in it for months and months. Old Ma Bowers went to see him but he was in Scunny and there weren't many buses so sometimes she went on the back of Mr Booth's Norton or in Jim Heals van. Only Pauls head was out of the iron tube and they fed him with a hosepipe. This is where he got interested in butterflies and moths. When he came out he had shrunk and his legs were dead little and he had leg irons. So he just sat in the old orchard doing nowt where there were loads of red admirals and peacocks and tiger moths etc. And then he tried to catch them with a net made out of stockings and then Old Ma Bowers got a book about butterfly collecting out of Epworth library and they did it.

The book was called Practical Entomology and they also got the Observers Book of British Butterflies. You have to sneak up on them and surprise them with a net from below. Then you put them in a killing jar which was a jam jar with some cotton wool and chloroform but they didn't have any so they got some wintergreen rubbing alcohol which Old Ma Bowers had some and it killed them and they went stiff. So you took them out with tweezers and put them in a relaxing box which was a biscuit tin with some sawdust from Jim Heals wood yard and meths and after two days you took them out and they were floppy. Then you had to mount them on a setting board. Jim Heals made some for Paul by sawing up cork board into 2x1 bits and chiselling a slit down the middle for the bodies of the moths and butterflies to fit in. Jim Heals lived next door in a wooden house in the woodyard. He was a joiner and carpenter and painter and decorator like his dad and grandad who had been there for hundreds of years in the same place. When they mixed paint they tried it out on the tool shed door.

There were thousands of colours and the paint had dried and was inches thick and was like stalactites and stalagmites in a waterfall. Old Ma Bowers said he was a confirmed bachelor.

So you put the butterfly and moths bodies into the slits in the cork boards and pinned them down their wings and legs etc with bits of torn up lavvy paper and pins and you left them for two weeks when they had gone stiff again and then Paul pinned them all in a box on the wall made also by Jim Heals and people came to look at them. The butterflies in the old orchard were red admirals and peacocks and tortoise shells and small coppers and cabbage whites but when they were all collected Paul and Old Ma Bowers went on hunting expeditions to the Turbary. Paul couldn't really walk with the leg irons not down the lane and the hospital wouldn't give him a wheelchair then so they got the old Triang kids Battlewagon in the Methodist Jumble sale and he went around in that as he was that small. Sometimes he went out exploring with Roy Booth spotting birds. He collected a painted lady and a common blue and cinnabars and Roy spotted a stonechat and got some owl pellets which are owl shit full of mouse bones. Everybody collected things for Paul Bowers. Kenny

Blanchard found some butterflies and moths dead in his dad's shit house but they were covered in spiderwebs and gone mouldy. The moths only came out at night and Old Ma Bowers and Paul tried to catch them around the lamp post near the bridge on the Drain with a net on a brush. The moths were like ghosts or vampires. Some looked like bats and were called hawks. There were elephant hawks that lived on the willow herb in the orchard and poplar hawks and privet hawks and there weren't many. Then they got the idea of making a moth trap.

And they got an old sheet and tied a washing line between two apple trees in the old orchard and hung up the sheet with pegs and at night put a torch behind it and next morning the moths were all asleep in the sheet. Everybody went round to look at the moths in the morning but there weren't that many either and then the battery ran out. This was when Audrey Glew had found the Death's Head Hawk in the seed potatoes in Barry Dodds field and the Epworth Bells said the Professor had the whole village in a flutter. Nobody ever called Paul Bowers the Professor before the Epworth Bells said he was.

The hospital wouldn't get Paul a wheelchair because they reckoned he wasn't badly enough so some people from The Wheatsheaf and the Wesley Chapel like Mrs Glew thought they would get money for one by having a collection at the Barrow Race like Dr Barnardos but for a wheelchair. The Barrow Race was because years ago Mart Twidale and Eric Boocock who worked on Common Farm had a bet in the Bridge Inn that they could race each other in a wheelbarrow all round the village having a pint in all the pubs. So they did it every year and not just Mart and Eric. You had two men and a wheelbarrow and one pushed and one sat in the barrow and they raced for five miles round the village past Grey Green along the top road and down Carr House Lane. The started at The Crown and then the Sir Solomon and then the Steers Arms then The Wheatsheaf and finished at the Bridge Inn and had a pint and swapped over pushers and riders every pub. Some ladies did it too so Old Ma Bowers and Joyce Booth did it with a sign collecting money for the wheelchair. Old Ma Bowers had done it before. It was all the farm lads from the village and some from Epworth and Crowle. There was a prize of a side of bacon. Everybody came out to watch and cheer and hung up the coronation flags. We all went round the crowd with collecting tins pulling Paul Bowers in the Battlewagon. Brian Robinson shouted new wheels for old etc. Everyone gave summat except some miserable old cow from Beltoft who said Paul should be put down. The last bit of the race was after The Wheatsheaf down Westgate to the Bridge Inn. The runners were all sweating and covered in beer and some had been sick. Everyone went mad when Old Ma Bowers and Joyce came past huffing and puffing. Ron Tex played a record out of his front room window. It was Great Balls of Fire by Jerry Lee Lewis.

At the Bridge Inn Howard Kirk and Olive Oil and

fat Raymond were there to give the prize. Gillian waved the winners flag and the winners were the two farm lads from Crowle. They got the side of bacon. Old Ma Bowers and Joyce Booth who won the women race didn't get owt but Howard Kirk said he would make up the money from the collection so Paul could get his wheelchair which was only right since it was his swimming pool to begin with. But his polio didn't get any better. Old Ma Bowers gave the Battlewagon to Brent Robinson and he went tearing round the village shunting into people with it.

Up the Rovers!

This all happened the season after seventeen year old wonder boy Alick Jeffrey had his leg broken in two places by a Frenchman when playing for England under 23s at Bristol. Alick was the most promising inside forward England had unearthed since the war and he played for the Rovers. And it was so out of the blue, so unexpected, such terrible bad luck on a boy with the soccer world at his feet. It happened this way. The 25000 crowd was hushed and tense, waiting to see whether Jeffrey or the young French centre forward would win a challenge for the ball. As they met in midfield everyone in the ground distinctly heard the sickening crack of the leg breaking. The Frenchman cried like a child after the match. It was a 0-0 draw.

Matt Busby had tried to sign him up for the Busby Babes but Rovers Irish manager Mr Peter Doherty wouldn't let him go so he stayed at Donny and scored over 23 goals and Rovers nearly went up. Also if he had gone to United he might have been dead.

We had all seen Alick play a load of times and he was our favourite as well as Harry Gregg and Charlie Williams who Old Ma Bowers said was a soap dodger. Ron

DONCASTER ROVERS

Back row, left to right:

J. Walker	H. Gregg
T. Ewing	R. Walker
M. Hunt	C. Williams
K. Hardwick,	B. Staton

Centre row, left to right:

P. Gavin	E. McMorran
H. Tindill	A. Jeffrey
J. Mooney	G. Walker

Front row, left to right:

J. Kilkenny	M. Connolly
L. Graham	R. Collinson

SOCCER BUBBLE GUM

Tex Robinson went into Donny on Saturdays to do some market business with electrical equipment and old records and building materials etc so a load of us went to Donny on his lorry for Rovers home games. Brian and Gordon went and Roy Booth and Kenny Blanchard from the

Little Turbary and Old Ma Bowers and Paul when he had got his wheelchair. We all had red and white scarves and rattles that Jim Heals had painted Up the Rovers on. We went to Bellevue in rain and shine. It was sixpence for boys and you could get in for nowt after half time and have Bovril but it was scalding. Some men had pies.

Bellevue was the first ground to have floodlights. We used to shout Put the candles on when it got dark in winter. Thousands of people used to go like when in the 3rd round of the FA cup we played West Brom at home and drew 1-1 then we were robbed 2-0 away at the Hawthorns. Also fat Raymond Kirk came to the Rovers when Howard Kirk took Raymond and Gillian to Donny on Saturdays when he was also going to the market and the Wellington Inn with some other farmers and masons. Also with Raymond was Fishy Addock from Armthorpe who went to Raymonds posh school whose sister was at Dora Cowley's school of dancing with Gillian Kirk. Fishy wasn't called Fishy because of fish. His dad didn't work down the pit in Armthorpe. He worked for the Yorkshire Coal Board. We used to stand behind Harry's goal except Paul Bowers who had a special place for spastics. At reserve matches when he had nothing to save Harry Gregg would talk to us and sign autographs and have a cigarette. He was playing for the reserves against Scarborough when he heard he had been picked for the Irish International team. Ginger Robinson had a big scrapbook of football autographs and pictures from newspapers including other teams.

Harry Gregg is the best goalkeeper in the world and that is true. He started out as understudy to the dependable veteran Ken Hardwick but after he got his Irish cap Mr Peter Doherty who was also Irish manager put him in the first team. After that Harry was very famous for his penalty saves. We used to shout Up the Rovers and Come on Charlie and Come on Flash and we would boo the ref who needed a white stick. Flash was Johnny Mooney who was bald and thin and looked weedy but was really fast and scored a fair few goals. Fat Raymond used to shout out rude things a lot like bum hole and bedwetter and make loud trumps. This made him and Fishy Addock laugh a lot until a St John's Ambulance man told them to Queen's word off. Fat Raymond also collected autographs which he bought off Ginger and told his posh friends that he had got them his sen. You could buy a ticket for the ball and if your number won you got the match ball but nobody ever did.

The team that season was Harry Gregg, Brian Makepeace from Rossington, Jimmy Kilkenny, Len Graham, Morgan Hunt from Askern, Billy Mordue, Pat Gavin, Flash Mooney, Charlie Williams, Tommy Cavanagh, Walter Kelly instead of Alick Jeffrey, Bert Tindill, Ronnie Walker and Geoff Walker who wasn't Big Ron's brother. The first game we all went to was Huddersfield.

When we got to Bellevue the first thing we saw was Alick Jeffrey getting out of a car on his crutches. He shook Paul Bowers hand in the wheelchair and Ginger got his autograph again and we all stroked his plaster for good luck. We lost 3-0. Charlie Williams wasn't playing because he had flu. Then we lost at Leyton away and Grimsby away and 5-0 at Middlesbrough away because of Brian Clough. When we played Middlesbrough at home we were bottom of Division Two played 7 won 1 lost 6 points 2 but Mr Doherty and the players were determined to shake off the effects of the unhappy start to the season and supporters can play their part in the fight to climb the League table by cheering their men on. And we beat them 3-2 with Flash Mooney and Walt Kelly and Tommy Ewing from the reserves all scoring goals and Ginger got Brian Clough's autograph. Harry had made some great saves and also when we drew away at West Ham in London making him the best goalkeeper in the country and also Ireland when Ireland beat England 3-2 at Wembley. At Fulham in London Charlie Williams scored an own goal when he deflected a centre into the net. By Bonfire Night Rovers had 7 points from 13 games. We needed 23 points from the next 29 games to stay up.

Bonfire Night started long before Bonfire Night. This was because we had to collect all the wood for the bonfire. Our bonfire was going to be on Barry Dodds's mouse field next to the Drain. We got wood from everywhere. Dead old branches, packing cases, old broken chairs, cardboard boxes from Fletchers shop etc. Howard Kirk was having one too so Freddie Swash and fat Raymond went out with the Massey Ferguson tractor and trailer and got loads of the best stuff from all the farmers like old roof beams and tree stumps from the thin snake wood. So Ron Tex Robinson went out with Brian at night in his lorry and they went to the old Sandtoft aerodrome and got big old doors from the hangars and tyres and some scaffolding planks and some fences just like the ones in Howard Kirk's field that Jim Heals made to teach Stargazer the jumping. Soon our bonfire was miles high. Bigger than Howard Kirk's.

Old Ma Bowers and Paul and Angela Whiteley made the guy. The guy was the Guy Forks scarecrow dummy that you burnt on the bonfire. The Guy Forks had tried to blow up the king with gunpowder in London but they had caught him and tortured him and burnt him alive which was what we did but with a scarecrow dummy on the bonfire. They had to get clothes for the guy so Angela got all the stuff left over from the Methodist Jumble Sale for nowt like a vest and shirt and socks and a tie etc. Old Ma Bowers got an old suit from Mrs Glew down Carr House Lane who had it in the back of the wardrobe since her husband died and that had been years ago and it was full of moth holes. And some boots and rubber gloves for hands. They made a body out of chicken wire and stuffed it with old newspapers and put all the clothes on and stuffed the pockets with some bangers. Then they made a head out of a bust old football and Angela painted a face on it and they got an old cap and made a beard out of old wool. It looked like Jimmy Hill the Fulham London inside right who scored two against us in the same game when Charlie Williams scored an own goal.

Angela Whiteley made a sign for Penny for the Guy and we got Jim Heals wheelbarrow and put Jimmy Hill in it and went all round the village to everywhere we had sold the dead mice for cats shouting Remember remember the fifth of november gunpowder treason and plot I see no reason why gunpowder treason should ever be forgot etc and penny for the guy. People came out to look at the guy and gave us pennies and sixpences. The money was for the fireworks. Roy Booth was in charge of buying the fireworks. He took the money and went to Scunny on the back of Mr Booths Norton because they had proper shops. Roy got a box of Standard fireworks with roman candles and golden showers and silver rain and air bombs and land mines and jumping jacks and catherine wheels and volcanoes and skyrockets and some sparklers and more bangers. We got some more bangers from Fletchers shop but these were for throwing on Mischief Night which was the night before Bonfire Night.

Mischief Night was when everybody did tricks and jokes on old people and you could do it and they couldn't get you for it because it was Mischief Night and allowed though some did get chased with a stick or a clip round the ear. The main thing was taking off peoples gates and swapping them over so everybody had the wrong gates. Then you put treacle on door knobs and tied dustbin lids to door knobs and knocked on doors and ran away. Then you put bangers in dustbins and rubbish in letterboxes. Some threw bangers at cats and dogs but we didn't. The other thing about Mischief Night was that you had to guard your bonfire because other people would set fire to it when you were doing mischiefing. Like the Beltoft gang. John Took guarded the bonfire with Mick the greyhound and his airgun with dum dum bullets. A couple of years back a lad had been burnt to death when he fell asleep and they set fire to his bonfire in Stainforth. They said it were gypos. You had to wait until it was ret dark on Bonfire Night before getting going.

There were millions of stars in the milky way and you could see the fire from the blast furnace at App Frod miles away in Scunny lighting up the sky. Barry Dodds was letting off the fireworks and lighting the bonfire. He had a big oil drum full of sand and a fireman's bucket and metal gloves. First we let off a big rocket to let everybody know we had started and we all got sparklers going and waved them about and Paul Bowers put some on his wheelchair. Then Barry Dodds lit the bonfire with paraffin and not petrol as it would have exploded.

When the Guy Forks went up in flames everyone cheered and shouted Remember remember the fifth of november again. Then all the bangers in his coat went off and all the dogs and pigeons went mad and a jumping jack banger chased Brent down the lane and Bri Robinson shouted great balls of fire. The fire went miles up into the sky and was dead hot and black smoke from the burning tyres. Angela Whiteley and her mam had cooked some bonfire parkin which was gingerbread and bonfire toffee which was treacle toffee which broke your teeth. Some people cooked potatoes in the bonfire but they went black and tasted of paraffin. Then Barry Dodds set off the fireworks. You had to light the blue touch paper and retire to a safe distance and there were hundreds of them and everybody from our end came and stood on the bridge. And cheered the sputnik rockets and roman candles and golden rains and the big catherine wheel that Ron Tex Robinson nailed to Fletchers gate. John Took had robbed a proper bird scarer from a potato field and threw it under the bridge and the bridge nearly blew up and loads of water soaked loads of people on the bridge and some rats came out too. It was dead late when it finished and some men went to The Wheatsheaf.

Howard Kirk's bonfire had burnt down on Mischief Night and he had to send Freddie Swash and fat Raymond out with the tractor and trailer to cadge some more wood and stuff off other farmers bonfires etc and he bought some good wood from Jim Heals woodyard which wouldn't burn. All the posh people came in their Jaguars and Armstrong Siddeleys and Rovers and Humber Snipes. A lad from fat Raymond's school burnt his hand off picking up a rocket and had to go to Scunthorpe Memorial Hospital.

The next home match we went to was when we beat Notts County 4-0. We all stood behind Harry's goal. He said hello and let us touch his cap for luck.

Charlie Williams played even having got a dislocated

collar bone in the draw with Lincoln and amateur Bircotes born Reece Nicholson came on and scored a goal also Flash Mooney, Big Ronnie Walker and Tommy Cavanagh. We were no longer bottom Swansea were bottom. Then we lost 2-0 away at Ipswich. This is what happened. Reece Nicholson was brought down in the penalty area when he was going to score so referee Mr Alfred Bond one of the best in the business had no hesitation in pointing to the penalty spot. Tommy Cavanagh took the kick but the Ipswich goalie saved it. It was a sorry business and Tommy was utterly dejected. Then Ipswich scored then got a penalty against Tommy for tripping up Doug Millward which he didn't do and it was yards outside the box anyway. What happened next was that Matt Busby tried to buy Harry Gregg for Manchester United for a load of money but Peter Doherty didn't want him to go and neither did the fans so they turned down the offer and Harry was going to play at home to Rotherham. But then the board of directors and masons got greedy and Matt Busby came to Donny and said he would pay 23,000 pounds which at the time was a world record for a goalkeeper and Harry said yes and so he went to the Busby Babes. So Peter Doherty bought a new goalkeeper from Sheffield United called Ted Burgin who had fully recovered from his broken leg for the Rotherham game. When he came on everybody booed and shouted for Harry and fat Raymond and Fishy shouted out bum head and silly clot etc and we didn't stand behind his goal but it did no good. Harry had gone. Then we lost twice to

Charlton over Christmas. Then Jimmy Kilkenny went into hospital with pneumonia. Then we lost 2-0 at home to Chelsea in the FA Cup 3rd round and we should have had a penalty when Walt Kelly was brought down but then we had a penalty and Tommy Cavanagh missed it. Ginger got Jimmy Greaves's autograph. Then Mr Peter Doherty left because he was fed up with them selling Harry and losing all the matches. So we didn't have a manager either. Then Bert Tindill and Tommy Cavanagh and Walt Kelly all said they wanted to leave too because they were fed up of losing all the matches. Then Ted Burgin broke his collar bone and we got Dave Macintosh.

Since Harry had joined the Busby Babes had won every game. On February 6th they beat Red Star Belgrade in Yugoslavia in the European cup. On the way home to England they stopped off at Munich in Germany in a snow storm and when the aeroplane took off again they skidded on the ice and the aeroplane crashed and exploded and everybody was killed. When we got out of school Old Ma Bowers had a Scunthorpe Star special evening paper. It had pictures of all the team and it said THE TEAM THAT DIED. Harry Gregg was dead. Some of us cried. Old Ma Bowers said it served him right for leaving the Rovers.

But Harry wasn't dead. Old Ma Bowers was lying. He was the hero of Munich. At first he thought he was dead but he woke up and pulled Bobby Charlton out then went back into the burning wreckage to pull out Jackie Blanchflower and Dennis Viollet and a baby. Who died was Tommy Taylor from Barnsley, David Pegg from Sheffield, Roger Byrne, Duncan Edwards who was brilliant, Billy Whelan, Eddie Coleman, Geoff Bent, Mark Jones. Then Harry came back and played in the FA Cup fifth round against Sheffield Wednesday and won 3-0. Then we went round saying we were United supporters. Our rattles were red and white and we said the Up the Rovers was Up the Rogers after United captain Roger Byrne who was now dead.

We all went to the Rovers away game with Barnsley. We got the bus from Donny bus station. We had liver and gravy and chips for dinner in Barnsley bus station. It was freezing and when we got to Oakwell the snow was coming down then it was a blizzard. By half time hundreds had gone home and we all had Bovril to stop shivering. We were covered in snow. In the second half it got so worse that you couldn't see the ball and the ref should have abandoned the game but he didn't. By the end we were the only people left in the ground as we couldn't go as the bus back to Donny wasn't until six o'clock. When they came off Big Ronnie gave us a big grin and others clapped us for staying. We drew 1-1. Then we lost 6-1 to Fulham at home. Jimmy Hill scored five of them. We should have used petrol. Ginger got Johnny Haynes and Tony Macedo's autographs but not Jimmy Hill even though he wanted to sign it. Then we were beaten away at Swansea 4-3 when Dave Macintosh went off with groin strain and

Billy Morgue fell over and the Swans got the last minute winner. Derby County beat us 2-1 at home when their first goal was offside then Blackburn beat us 5-1 at home with internationals Ron Clayton and Bryan Douglas and Ginger got all their autographs when he sneaked on to the team bus. Then we were beaten 3-1 by Sheffield United away then 3-2 away at Blackburn although Ronnie Walker scored with a 25 yard pile driver. Our new goalie Willy Nimmo played his first game for Rovers at home v Lincoln but we still lost 3-1. The last game of the season was Ipswich Town at home. We had to win to stay up. We drew 1-1. Everybody was sad but we cheered the Rovers off the pitch. Some people shouted that Rovers were shit including fat Raymond then Kenny Blanchard gave him a chinese burn. We were relegated to the Third Division as we were bottom. Played 42 Won 8 Drawn 11 Lost 23 Points 27. The next week was the Cup Final.

Manchester Manchester Manchester United if they win on Saturday they deserve to be knighted. Since Old Ma Bowers had lied about Harry Gregg being dead the Busby Babes had risen from the flames of the Munich disaster to the Cup Final at Wembley. It was a footballing miracle. Harry and Bill Foulkes who got out of the plane were in the team with Bobby Charlton and Dennis Viollet who were injured in it. Also Ernie Taylor from Blackpool. Matt Busby had got out of hospital in Germany to be there. Bolton Wanderers were led by England captain and centre forward Nat Lofthouse. We all went to Robinsons to watch it on TV. Ron Texs TV was the only one in our end of the village. It was big and he said he had won it in a Dr Barnardos raffle. Some farm men came too and some dads too etc. They had got crates of Watneys pale ale. There were a hundred thousand people there and before the game we all sang Abide with me. When Harry came on with the team that refused to die we all cheered and rattled our Up the Rogers rattles. Paul Bowers had made a cardboard and silver paper FA Cup with Up Red Devils written on it. Then they sang God Save the Queen. Nat Lofthouse scored for Bolton after about one minute. It wasn't Harry's fault. Then Bobby Charlton hit the bar and Harry made loads of saves. At half time everybody had pop and crisps. In the second half United went on the attack until Nat Lofthouse shoulder charged Harry into the back of the net with the ball. It was never a goal. It was a bloody foul. It was cheating. Harry was knocked out but the ref said it was a goal. He had been bribed. And Bolton won 2-0 and the dream was over. Ron Tex and the farm men all went to The Wheatsheaf and had double diamonds with Uncle Walter and we sat on the bridge until it got dark then went home.

Kenny Blanchard sent a letter to Nat Lofthouse at Bolton saying that it was a foul and he was a lying cheating bugger and he had been bribed and if he ever came to Donny he would get murdered. Kenny was scared for ages that the the Police would come and put him in borstal but then he got a letter from Bolton Wanderers saying Dear

Kenneth thank you for your interest in Bolton Wanderers Football Club and a picture of the team with printed autographs. He sold the autographs to fat Raymond for two and six and wiped his bum on the letter. Then Harry went off to play for Ireland in the World Cup in Sweden with manager Peter Doherty and turned the football world upside down and defied all odds when they got to the quarter final after beating Czechoslovakia. Harry Gregg won the best goalkeeper in the world prize so in the end it was a victory for the mighty Donny Rovers.

The Special Rabbits

This is not about the special rabbits. It's about secrets. This we didn't know then. Howard Kirk was born in a pigsty in poverty in Epworth. His father was a farm worker and he bred litters of pigs that lived in the house with Howard and his five brothers Herbert, Harry, Walter, Arthur and George but Herbert died of the pigs. Howard wanted to play the harmonica in the Excelsior Minstrels in Cleethorpes but they wouldn't let him so he went to be a blacksmith's boy and then a blacksmith and then got married to the wife nobody knows nowt about and moved to the village to be a farmer and made something of his sen. Then he got some fields and Common Farm and some others. Then the first Mrs Kirk died and Howard got another wife from the village called Grace because by now he had a bit of money and was an Agricultural Merchant etc. They had Fran and went to Bridlington where they saw George Formby and met Olive Oil who was a fever nurse who had got smallpox and was in Bridlington to get better with the sea air. Olive Oil was not from around here.

Howard and Grace got Olive Oil to come to Common Farm to look after Fran and be a friend to Grace as Howard was always doing the ploughing. This was alright for a bit and then Olive and Grace got the idea of making a bit of money for their sens by breeding the special rabbits. They found a broken old LNER third class railway carriage that had been standing in a bed of nettles for years in a siding near Ealand and Howard Kirk dragged it to the field with his tractor and they pulled out all the seats and luggage racks and painted it green. Then they hung up a board saying Grace and Olives Rabbitry. Then they got some old cages from the hen house and got some rabbits from Gainsborough.

The first rabbits were Rex rabbits and they got a blue buck and a piebald doe and put them to mate and soon had loads which they didn't sell for meat but to the pet shop in Scunny for kids pets. Then they got some special Flemish Giants and Loppy Ears rabbits that they called Flopsy, Mopsy and Cotton Tail which are rare breed and bred some of those and sold the special babies to people who wanted special rabbits in Fur and Feather. It was hard work cleaning them out and giving them rabbit food and mating them and Fran had to help. Then they put the Loppy Ears and the Flemish Giants into the fancy livestock section of Epworth and District Agricultural Show where they also had fancy guinea pigs and ferrets and bantams and won some first prize rosettes and prize money and then they went to the Brigg Show and the Selby Show in Grace's Morris Traveller and won some more rosettes and cups and money. It took hours of grooming the rabbits but they did this for years and were happy.

Then Grace got sick and had to go to bed and Olive Oil had to nurse her and look after Fran and Howard really. Fran got the munk on and didn't want to clean out the rabbit cages anymore or feed them so Howard took them all and sold them on Donny Market for nowt which made Olive Oil unhappy.

Then Grace died and Old Ma Bowers reckoned it were myxomatosis and Fran had enough and went to Kettering to be a nurse. Olive Oil had burnt her boats in Northallerton and people were starting to talk as she was a lady alone with Howard Kirk in Common Farm who was sad but getting over it. After a bit Olive Oil said she would marry Howard and be his third wife after he said he didn't want any babies and she didn't either and he had plenty of money. So they did and went to Bridlington for their honeymoon where George Formby was on again. Then they had Gillian who was a girl and Olive Oil was very unhappy and couldn't look after her so Fran had to come back from nursing in Kettering to help out and she wasn't happy either so they got Mrs Glew as a servant. Old Ma Bowers said that something queer had gone on and it did again when Olive Oil began to have another baby she didn't want. So Howard Kirk went mad.

One night he went into baby Gillian's room and rubbed shit all over the walls then he took all his clothes off and ran up the village waving his arms about shouting summat about potatoes. Freddie Swash had to go and get him but Howard punched him in the gob. In the end some others got Howard back to the farm and Doctor Mitchell came and said he had a nervous breakdown and gave him some knockout drops. Then they wanted to put him in a nursing home in Lincoln called the Retreat which was a loony bin you paid for but he wouldn't go. Then his brother Uncle Walter and Olive Oil told him that George Formby was in there and then he wanted to go so they took him there in Walter's Ford Popular and left him there. They gave Howard electric shocks that burnt his brains and put him in cold baths etc and when he got home he was never the same again and fat Raymond had been born and Olive Oil was stuck with him forever.

All this happened ages ago and now Howard Kirk had loads more money and he was chairman of the Isle of Axholme NFU even though he didn't say much and he gave money for the Barrow Race and the Haxey Hood etc and masons but Olive Oil was still a miserable cow. And he was President of the Epworth and District Agricultural Show.

The Epworth Show was every summer in the Epworth Show ground on Wroot road where there were football pitches for the rest of the time. They had lots of stuff. There were tents all round a big circle where they had pony competitions and show jumping and a motorbike display and best cattle and carthorses and a sheepdog display and a parade of tractors, scots dancing etc.

One year they had the wrestling and that is the year we all went and this happened. Around the ring there were loads of tents and competitions. There was a flower show and a vegetables and fruit show and fancy livestock show with special rabbits budgerigars and hens and ferrets etc and a cake baking show. You could win prizes of money and cups. Then there was a beer tent and a tea tent where you could get sandwiches and buns and a tent selling animal feed and fertiliser and pitchforks. There was an Andy Pandy roundabout for kids like Brent Robinson and Kenny Blanchard got on it and nearly bust it.

In the middle was the President's tent where Howard Kirk sat with a flower in his button hole smoking his cigar with Olive Oil who was miserable but doing her best. They had crates of free beer and special sherry and gin and seats and tables and piles of free food for the posh guests which were other farmers and masons and the mayor and Major Stubley from Skellow and people from the canning factory in Selby and wives in big hats and they all got drunk. This was Howard Kirks big day as Gillian was in the junior show jumping with Stargazer. They had been up all night cleaning the pony and polishing its tackle and hoofs and washing his tail etc and Freddie Swash had arrived early with Stargazer and Gillian in the horsebox. Gillian had jodhpurs and a hunting jacket and a crash helmet. Fat Raymond did nowt. We all thought we would have a go at winning a bit of money in competitions. Roy Booth put his fantails in the fancy pigeon show. Paul Bowers made some cheese scones for the mens baking show and we all did the fancy dress show but not John Took who said it was babyish. He was going to put Mick in the Dog Show but Mick had the scar and a limp so he left him at home. First off was the Armthorpe Colliery brass band playing a selection of airs and marches and then the Royal Signals motorbike display team rode around dead fast in circles just missing each other and then did it no hands and stood on the seats and then jumped over hay bales and a ring of fire and then made a human pyramid on just one bike. They all had 750CC Triumph Tigers and white crash helmets. The air smelled of burning rubber and two stroke. Then they put up the jumps of poles and planks and gates and some were high and wide and they had flowers on them in barrels and a wall made out of wood bricks.

The jumpers had come from miles away like Kirton Lindsey and they all had money. They were mostly girls because of Pat Smythe. There was a posh lad from Bessacarr called Sam Masarella who was at Raymond's posh school and had been at the caterpillar swimming party. His dad was Masarellas ice cream and they had a van at the show where you could get cornets and tubs and sandwich wafers and choc ices. Sam Masarella's pony was called Raspberry Ripple and he had won loads of jumping cups from all over the place. Sam saw Raymond and said what are you doing here you fat lout so Raymond spat at his horse. When Stargazer came on to jump everyone cheered like crazy. When Sam Masarella came on to jump everyone booed and made snobby noises. Gillian got twelve faults which was not fair as she only knocked down three fences a gate and the wood wall and half went into the water. Sam Masarella got a clean round and a big cup and Gillian got a yellow rosette for coming third. Howard Kirk was as pleased as punch and Gillian was the apple of his eye and it had been worth all the sacrifices. Gillian walked around wearing her rosette, a silly grin and muddy jodhpurs. While all this was carrying on fat Raymond let down the tyres of Masarellas horsebox. Then they paraded all the highland cows and sheep and tractors and shetland ponies so we went off to see if we had won owt. Roy Booths fantails hadn't won but got a recommended which was good as there were some amazing pigeons like Jacobins and Frill backs and some with hairy feet. There were some fancy budgies and cockatoos and special rabbits like Olive used to have and special hens like Rhode Island Reds and Silkies. Paul Bowers cheese scones came nowhere but Mrs Glew got first for turnips and Old Ma Bowers for her crab apple jelly from the old orchard and Jim Heals won a prize in the handicrafts for a carved pipe rack. Then it was time for the Fancy Dress competition.

Bri Robinson was Cliff Richard. He had painted on sidies and Ron Tex's purple ted jacket which was miles too big for him and a bootlace tie made of a bootlace and he had made a guitar out of cardboard with High Class Baby painted on. Ginger was Lady Docker who was a millionaire lady who lived in Monty Carlo and was in the papers. He had his mams dress and a manky fur rug he found in a bin. He had some jewellery made out of Christmas tree decorations and red lipstick and a head scarf. He looked ret good and walked around like a lady all day. Paul Bowers was the Tin Man. Old Ma Bowers had got some paint tins from Jim Heals and they painted them like tin and hung them around Paul and the wheelchair and on his head and John Took pushed him and it made a clanking noise like the real tin man. Angela was Shirley Temple. She had her hair done curly and had a frilly dress and a lollipop. Kenny Blanchard dressed up like Harry Gregg with shorts and a green jumper and a bandage round his head. He also had his Up the Rogers rattle which was daft as Harry never had a rattle. Also there was a cowboy, a golliwog and a spider. The spider won and Paul came second and won five shilling and then we had to walk all around the pony ring when they had cleared out the highland cattle and shetland ponies and boy scouts and have our pictures took by the Epworth Bells. Paul spent his prize on some proper chloroform to kill his butterflies.

Then it was time for the Wrestling. This was the first time they had the wrestling and they didn't have it again.

They had put up a wrestling ring in the middle of the field and everybody pushed in close even Old Ma Bowers and Mrs Glew etc who had seen it in Bridlington and liked it. They had found some floodlights too. It was an all star treat for the grapple fans. There were fights with Big Bomber Bates v Count Bartelli and Pepi and Koki the Belgian midgets and Leon Aris the Barnsley Barndoor v DJ Jimmy Savile from Leeds. Count Bartelli had a mask and had never been unmasked. It was two falls one submission or a knock out to decide the winner. Big Bomber Bates was a Lancashire bomber pilot in the war and he was also the masked Ghoul sometimes. They rang the bell and the Bomber gave Bartelli a forearm smash to the kidneys and a rabbit chop and and then got him in an armlock but he wouldn't submit and the Count turned it into a whip and the Bomber went head over heels out of the ring and some women hit him with a handbag and he got back in but the Count tied him up in the ropes and then kicked him in the face but the Bomber grabbed him by the mask and got him in a double nelson and smashed him into the ring post and then he went down and the Bomber sat on his belly and the ref counted three and that was the first fall so they went back to the corners but Count Bartelli got a bucket of water and threw it all over the Bomber but missed and hit the referee who fell over and the Count danced around the ring and everyone booed and cheered and fat Raymond shouted nappy rash. Round two the Bomber got the Count in a scissors hold like Roy Booth did on John Took about the eggs but the Count grabbed the Bombers hair and pulled him around the ring by his hair and then chopped his throat. Then the Count got him in an aeroplane spin and chucked him out of the ring and then there was a gigantic thunder storm with thunder and lightning and rain coming down like stair rods and hail stones as big as conkers and a huge wind and we never found out who won. Everyone ran into the beer tent or the food tent or Howard Kirks tent. You could hear the rain battering the tent roof like tommy guns.

We ran into the beer tent which was hot and sweaty and smelt of sick and steam was coming off the tarpaulin and loads of men were saying they'd seen nowt like it in their life etc. Then the Count and other wrestlers ran in and when Pepi and Koki came in everybody sang Hi ho hi its off to work we go and laughed and Pepi and Koki told them to Queen's word off in squeaky foreign voices and everybody laughed loads more. We were packed in like sardines. You couldn't breathe. Then the wrestler DJ Jimmy Savile who was a daft lad from Leeds put his hand up Angela Whiteleys frock and she bit him and he had to go to St John's Ambulance.

When it stopped the whole show ground was under water. Some tents had blown over and all the flags from the coronation had come down and the cables and floodlights were sparking. The field was nowt but mud. Nobody had wellies. All the cars were stuck and the horseboxes. Everybody had to help to push them out and got the tractors from the tractor display and some tow ropes and the police came to sort it out and they got the tow truck from Barry Dodd at Selwyn Motors in. Howard Kirk had to look after it all cos he was the President. Everybody helped to get Stargazers horsebox out but the Masarellas horse box tilted over and Raspberry Ripple went mad and kicked the sides of the box in and they nearly had to fetch the vet. It took all night to get all the cars and vans out. Some were there next day. They had to reseed the whole field before the football season started.

Ron Tex Robinson picked all our lot up in his lorry and we went home in the back and we sang a song about if you miss this one there'll never be another one, last train to San Fernando.

The Temple of Doom

When we all had bikes we went on bike rides as far as Owston Ferry etc. We all had push bikes except Paul Bowers and Brent. They were old second hand grids like Raleighs and Hercules and we fixed them up and mended the chains and Barry Dodds helped us. He had a soldering iron. Roy Booth had stormy archer gears and a saddlebag and John Took had drop down racing handlebars. We biked to Lindholme Lake with Roy Booth to see a grebe because someone said there was one there but it wasn't there. Ginger Robinson had a girls bike so did Angela Whiteley. Also where we went on the bikes when there was no Rovers was to Saturday morning pictures at the Rio in Epworth. It cost sixpence to get in. It was always packed with loads of kids from all the villages and

Epworth and some louts like the Beltoft gang. You had to wait outside til it opened and then everybody charged to get in and tried to get on the front row of the balcony where you could throw stuff down on the kids downstairs. The Beltoft gang once threw a kid off it. Sometimes John Took got in first and went to the gents lavvy and let everybody in through the window without paying. Then everybody had to sing the ABC Miners song:

We are the boys and girls of the well known miners of the ABC.

Such a happy crowd are we.

All pals together at the ABC.

Then everybody would cheer and shout and then the manager Mr Sydney Yorke came on and shouted for them all to shut up or there would be no pictures so they did and the lights went down and then everyone was excited and cheered again. Then they had cartoons like Tom and Jerry and Bugs Bunny and Popeye the Sailor man with Olive Oil which was why we called Howard Kirks wife Olive Oil because she was called Olive and was tall and skinny and mardy.

Then they would have Abbott and Costello on or the Three Stooges who were daft and the Goose steps out with Will Hay. Then they had an interval and sold Masarellas ice cream and lollipops and everybody threw it around and off of the balcony down kids necks. Then there was a film about the Queen and joining the Navy and a cowboy like Hopalong Cassidy or the Cisco kid or Flash Gordon in

Space fighting Ming the merciless on the Planet Mongo. Or Zorro.

When it was Zorro everyone came out sword fighting for weeks.

Once there was Reach for the Sky about Douglas Bader who lived in Sprotbrough outside Donny near where Howard Kirk had bought another farm at Cadeby and Freddie Swash was going to be farm manager. Douglas Bader was a local war hero who was sporty and good humoured with a buoyant zest for life and flying. After playing some cricket he went into the airforce and did loop the loops and upside down flying in a Bristol Bulldog with two wings. One day he had a bad crash and they had to cut his legs off. Then he was in hospital with a nurse etc. When the war broke out he joined the battle of Britain fighting the Jerrys in spitfires with false metal legs and he shot down hundreds of Nazi messerschmitts. Then he was shot down in flames and bailed out on a parachute and left his leg in the burning spitfire. The Jerrys put him in Colditz prison camp and Winston Churchill got the airforce to parachute him a new leg. When he put it on he tried to escape but didn't. So he was a beacon of hope among the clouds of doom. People in Sprotbrough reckoned he was big headed but that's Sprotbrough for you.

On the way back from the pictures we were coming round the turn by the railway crossing when Freddie Swash came racing past in his shitty Cortina and knocked Brian Robinson off his bike and drove off parping his hooter.

Brian had a grazed knee and a cut on his head and a bent front wheel and had to push it home and said he was going to get Freddie Swash.

Back at our end everybody made Douglas Bader parachutes out of hankys and string and tied toy soldiers to them but they got stuck in the telephone wires where the swallows sit before they migrate to Africa and hung there all winter and some fell in the Drain. Then everybody wanted to do parachuting jumps. In the lane down to the Little Turbary where Kenny Blanchard's house was and before you got to the pig woman's house was the field where the gypos camped when they came to do pea and potato picking etc. There was a big old brick barn that had been there for hundreds of years. It was what was left of a farm that had shut down years ago after the foot and mouth. It was a wreck but part of it was the barn full of straw bales for cattle feed piled up to the roof. Roy Booth had seen it looking for barn owls and this was where he found the barn owl pellets so there were some there. Some of the straw bales had broken all over the floor so you could climb up to the beams and jump off into the straw parachuting. John Took swung on the beams like Tarzan of the apes. Everyone did jumping and forward rolls. It were great. Roy pushed Paul Bowers down to the barn in the wheelchair looking for butterfly cocoons and John said with Paul here they should do the bit in the film when Winston Churchill parachuted Douglas Bader's leg into Colditz. So they made a big parachute out of potato sacks and binder twine and Paul took off his leg iron and they tied it to the parachute and John climbed up to the roof of the barn and chucked it off. It crashed to the ground and got bent. John Took's dad give him a leathering because he had to pay to get the leg fixed and said he would send him to Borstal in Hatfield.

This was when there was pig rustling which was like the cattle rustling bandits in the wild west at the pictures but with pigs. The pig woman on the end of the Little Turbary had lost a sow and a litter when some men with a van stole them at midnight with masks on like Zorro but she couldn't stop them and they pushed her over. She lived with the pigs in the house like Howard Kirk had and did her own slaughtering and butchering on a big old door. She slit their throats and and drained all the blood and made black puddings and chopped them up with a saw and made sausages and chops and pigs feet and ears and heads and brawn and polony etc and sold them to the butchers and in The Wheatsheaf. You made ham and bacon by hanging half a pig on a hook in the pantry next to the range with a cloth round it to keep out the flies and wasps. Then a year later you had ham and bacon. Everybody had hooks in the pantry. Many farmers and masons had pigs rustled so there was a reward for rounding up the pig rustlers. So everybody looked for clues everywhere for weeks but never found any. Old Ma Bowers said it were gypos or the squatters.

Kenny Blanchard built a den in the parachute barn in the straw bales. He piled them up to make a secret room and put down sacks as a floor and made a roof out of corrugated iron and put more bales on top. Then he made a front door and a secret back passage and a spy hole. It was pitch black and hot as hell in there and you needed a torch. A lad in Louth had made a straw den and gone in with a candle and burnt his sen to death. This was where Kenny hid his secret books about geography. He was in the den when a car pulled up in the old fold yard and he looked out of the spy hole and it was Freddie Swash in his shitty Cortina. Freddie got out and had a cigarette and then a van pulled up and parked where Kenny couldn't see and then Freddie walked over to the van. After a bit Kenny said he heard grunting of pigs and squeals. Then Freddie got back in the Cortina and drove off like lightning. So Freddie was head of the pig rustling bandits. Brian Robinson was rct pleased when Kenny told everybody what had happened as everybody knew that it was Freddie Swash that grassed to the police about Brian's dad Ron Tex and the lead from the Wesleyan Chapel roof that got him six months in Donny prison. So now Freddie would go to prison over the pigs and he wouldn't get the farm managers job off of Howard Kirk in Cadeby and it would serve him right and Kenny would get the reward. But Roy Booth said we had to have proper evidence and catch them redhanded. So everyone had to take turns to follow Freddie on the bikes to see where he was going.

Freddie didn't go anywhere much for ages except Common Farm and his bungalow where he lived with his mam and Clay Bank Farm and South Carr Farm and a lorry load of washed carrots to Goole and The Wheatsheaf and the Bridge Inn and the Steers Arms and the Sir Solomon near the war memorial at the other end of the village where Joyce Booth puked up in the Barrow Race and where they had the Fair. Then one night Freddie was in the Sir Solomon and Ginger Robinson was on watch and when it got dark Freddie got into his Cortina and instead of going to his bungalow he went the other road past the railway station and then he stopped and looked around to see of anyone was about and then drove in through the stone gates of Temple Belwood. Then a van went through the gates too. But Ginger had to go home for his tea so he couldn't go in and see what was going off. Temple Belwood was a big wrecked castle that was hundreds of years old and was falling down. It had been where Temple Knights and monks lived a thousand years ago but then it was the Lord of the Manner who had a horse called Sir Solomon that broke his leg when they went out hunting and had to be shot. Then it was a prison then a posh hotel with dancing but nobody went so then it was empty for years and then the roof fell in and a tree grew through it. Now it was overgrown with weeds and brambles and nettles etc and it was dangerous because bits kept falling off and bats lived there. Like Dracula. People went there blackberry picking and for conkers. Roy Booth had been there birdwatching to see a sparrow hawk which was there. People were scared to go there at night because there were strange lights and noises and it was haunted by the dead monks but Old Ma Bowers said it wasn't ghosts it was courting couples. Brian Robinson said it was because of the ghosts scaring people away at night that Freddie and his gang were taking the rustled pigs there to sell them on. So they had to catch him at it and get evidence.

Paul Bowers had a Brownie camera with a battery flash for taking pictures of his moths etc he lent to Brian to get the evidence as he couldn't go to catch Freddie in his wheelchair his sen. They told Old Ma Bowers they were going to take pictures of the bats. Old Ma Bowers said the bats could get stuck in your hair and you would have to get it shaved off with a razor. Angela Whiteley couldn't go as she had to stay and guard the pig lady pigs except they had been rustled already. John Took still wasn't allowed out. Nobody was scared of the ghosts as they were always men in sheets. So this time Brian was on stake out outside the Sir Solomon horse pub and Ginger and Roy and Kenny Blanchard were hiding behind the wall with their bikes. Roy Booth had the camera and flash bulbs in his saddle-bag. When it got dark Freddie came out of the pub and drove off in his shitty Cortina to Temple Belwood. Bri got on his bike and signalled everybody and they followed Bri down the lane and to the gate of the Temple where they switched their bike lamps off so the rustlers wouldn't see them coming. It was pitch black. There was an Owl. When they got near they got off the bikes and hid behind a hedge. Freddie was out of his car having a cigarette. Roy put the flash bulb in. Then a van came down the lane and flashed its lights. It was Jim Heals van. There wasn't much room for that many pigs.

Jim got out and rolled a cigarette and said nah then and then Freddie and Jim got in the back of Jim's van and shut the doors. Brian Robinson got the camera and crawled like a snake to the back of the van and looked through the window and took a photo but the flash didn't go off. Then they all got back on the bikes and raced back down the lane. Brian was laughing his head off. They all stopped at the War Memorial and Brian told them he hadn't seen any pigs but Freddie Swash was showing Jim Heals his bum. Which was rude. Then Freddie came past slowly in his Cortina followed by Jim in his van. They must have seen them but didn't say owt. So everybody went and had some chips.

Nobody knew what to do about Freddie Swash's bottom. They didn't tell anybody except John Took and Paul Bowers when they took his camera back with the flat battery. They told Old Ma Bowers that they hadn't seen any bats. They didn't tell Angela Whiteley. Kenny said there were men showing their bottoms in one of his secret books. Roy Booth took the film to the chemists but there was nowt on it except some pictures of caterpillars on a leaf and they were all fuzzy. It said in the Epworth Bells that they had caught the pig rustlers. It was the farm lads from Crowle that won the Barrow Race. They must have been scouting out where all the pigs were. So it weren't Freddie Swash and Kenny didn't get the reward. Fat Raymond said that Howard Kirk and the farmers had gone round their house and kicked their teeth in. So Brian Robinson had not got Freddie this time but Freddie was now very nice to us and bought us spice and pop and Jim Heals give us the wood for the goalposts.

The Mighty Sparrow Hawks

Kenny Blanchard lived on the Turbary. He hadn't been here long. This was the Little Turbary not the Big Turbary. You went down the lane along the Dyke but the other way from Roy Booths pigeon loft. You went past the wrecked parachuting barn and then some fields and hedges and at the end was the pig woman's pigsty who had her pigs rustled and had put barbed wire up. Not many people lived on the Turbary as it was only flat scabby fields and ditches but some smallholdings where people grew vegetables and had dogs and some sheep. There was a man who sold puppies of alsatians. There were no trees but there were some blackbirds and peewits and skylarks. Also in the sky were the nuclear Vulcan bombers from RAF Finningley where they kept the atom bombs to bomb Russia. Kenny Blanchard had moved there not long ago with his dad from Grimsby when his mam died and he got a job at Keadby power station.

Kenny's dad was called Keith. Kenny's dad had worked on the fish docks and had a trial for the Mariners but nowt came of it. He was very sad so he came here to get away from it. Kenny had to do all the housework and cooking as his dad was at the power station working. He had a BSA. Kenny's house was like a small farm and had an outside toilet and a shed where his dad grew some bulbs. There was a scabby field and this was where we played football until it got dark and we had to bike home in the dark. Kenny's dad painted a goal on the wall of the outside lav with whitewash. We took it in turns to play Harry Gregg and Flash Mooney. Or Billy Wright from Wolves who was England captain and married the one in the Beverley Sisters. Or Alfredo Di Stefano from Real Madrid. Sometimes Kenny's dad played too but not much. Paul Bowers used to come and watch with Old Ma Bowers. Paul tried to kick the ball but was shit and fell over. But Paul Bowers wasn't shit at Subbuteo. This was the game you played with plastic players on your table and you flicked them and had goals and a referee etc. You had a marked out pitch and the goalies were on sticks and Paul put sticky tape in the goals so the ball stuck. Paul and Old Ma Bowers played it every night when there were no butterflies or moth. Roy Booth and Jim Heals played too. And Angela Whiteley. You could get different teams but not the Rovers so Paul had Man U and also Blackpool. They had made a stadium and some stands out of cardboard and some floodlights and everything and they had a league and a Cup Final and everything. Roy Booth said Subbuteo was small buzzard in foreign latin which was just daft.

The season after Rovers got relegated to Div Three and Munich was another unfortunate season for the Rovers. Alick Jeffrey still wasn't fit but we had a new manager Mr Jack Crayston, formally of Arsenal who was the type of manager we want, while he in turn knows what he wants and will do all he can do achieve the desired results. We lost the first game 3-0 away to Tranmere Rovers who were lucky to be promoted. With his wide knowledge of the game Mr Jack Crayston was able to pinpoint the defects in the match at Prenton Park and supporters could depend on it that he will do all in his power to remedy any recurring weaknesses in the future. The first home game we went to in Ron Tex's lorry was Stockport County at home where we won 4-1. We stood behind Willy Nimmo's goal except fat Raymond and Fishy who had got season tickets in the stand that Howard Kirk had paid for. Good riddance to bad rubbish. Then we beat Brentford away and lost to Reading away and beat QPR at home. The Rovers were back. Then we lost to QPR away 3-1 and Bournemouth away 1-0 when Tommy Cavanagh was injured and Jimmy Kilkenny had to go to right half and Big Ron had to go to left half and Willy was definitely off the ground when he was shoulder charged into the net. Then Plymouth Argyle away 4-0 and Norwich at home 1-0. By the time we played Plymouth at home we had played 10 won 4 drawn 0 lost 6 and were 4th from bottom. Ginger stopped getting autographs as there was nobody any good. We all went to the Plymouth home game including fat Raymond and Fishy who had been told off in the stands for shouting things like BO and hairy donkey. The first half was brilliant and Rovers were winning 4-2 at half time with two goals from Big Ron Walker and one each from Johnnie Meredith and Len Graham. Plymouth scored four in the second half so we lost 4-6 and then we lost 5-0 away to Southend. By the time of the next home game with Bury Mr Jack Crayston was running out of players as Brian Makepeace, Flash Mooney and Peter Higham were all injured so we only had 4 forwards. We lost 1-0 and then we lost to Mansfield and then Kenny Blanchard had the idea of starting our own team.

The idea was to have 7 a side which would be Kenny and Brian and Ginger Robinson and Roy Booth and John Took and a kid called Cyril Tonkinson he knew who had moved down Carr House and could play a bit. Fat Raymond wanted to be in too but only if he played in goal. He said he was keeper in his posh school team and had saved loads. We didn't want him but Kenny reckoned his dad might give us some money. Brent could be the mascot. The home stadium would be Kenny's field and Kenny's dad would be manager but he didn't want to be but he would be referee. Kenny was captain because it was his field. When

Old Ma Bowers found out from Roy Booth she said she and Paul should be manager because of the Subbuteo league and they were. Everyone had to work to build the pitch. They had to scythe down all the long grass and thistles and nettles and pull out all the big stones and rocks then pick up all the broken bottles and dog shit and sheep shit. Roy Booth found a rooks skull. It took ages but sometimes they had pop and crisps. Old Ma Bowers made some Kraft cheese sandwiches etc. Then they lent a lawnmower off of a man off of the allotments and put down some grass seeds where it was just bare mud but they never came up. Then they got some goalposts off Jim Heals who cut up some telegraph poles. He had to dig deep holes and bash the poles down with a lump hammer and they all fitted on the cross bar with big nails and thick rope. Then they made some nets out of chicken wire that Freddie Swash brought from Common Farm with fat Raymond from when they had chickens. Freddie Swash didn't say owt and neither did we. Then we painted the lines on the pitch with special whitewash. And the goalposts. It was a bit short and a funny shape and the moles kept digging it up.

Kenny wanted to call the team Blanchard Rovers. John Took wanted the Belton Gunners. Brian wanted Axholme Adders. Ginger wanted to call the team Turbary Sports Verein from Eintracht Frankfurt SV from the European Cup with Real Madrid but Old Ma Bowers said she wasn't a bloody Jerry and they weren't a sports club anyway. Then Cyril Tonkinson says what about Westgate

Wednesday after Sheffield Wednesday and everybody liked that except John Took. Then Roy Booth said that Sheffield Wednesday were the Owls then they had to have nickname and said the Sparrow Hawks and everyone liked that even John Took. Everybody had hob nail leather boots with studs you had to dubbin. Fat Raymond had some special Ronnie Clayton continental boots but he was a spoilt brat. Angela and Old Ma Bowers got some shirts from the Wesleyan Jumble Sale. They were long sleeves and short sleeves and vests and they died them green in the copper with some die they got from Fletchers shop but it didn't look the same as on the packet. They were meant to be red but Fletchers had run out. It would've come out pink anyway. Fat Raymond had a green jumper and some special goalkeeper gloves and a cap. They made some green and white badges cut out of a tablecloth with BT on them and drew a sparrow hawk on them.

Old Ma Bowers got some fixtures. Mr Nolan at the school had a team called Nolan's Juniors and the Sparrow hawks would play them home and away and then there was the Epworth lads who played in the Epworth Show pitch. So we had two League fixtures and then we needed an FA Cup Final. Jim Heals knew the landlord of the Gun and Duck in West Butterwick and he said he would get up a team. So the Final was home and away on a Friday and a Saturday. First at Kennys and then at West Butterwick. Kenny and Ginger Gordon made some posters.

GRAND OPENING MATCH
AT THE KENNY BLANCHARD TURBARY STADIUM.
WESTGATE WEDNESDAY V MR NOLANS JUNIORS.
SATURDAY, 3 OCLOCK. COFFEE.

And put them on some trees and telegraph poles and in Fletchers window. Paul Bowers had a John Bull printing kit so he printed up some postcards about the match etc and everyone posted them through doors all over the village. Brian Robinson made a postcard saying MR JORDAN is a CISSY and posted it through Jordan's letterbox. Jordan was the headmaster who give everybody the cane. Old Ma Bowers got everybody to do training so Kenny's dad Keith did the training as he once nearly played for Grimsby Town which is near Cleethorpes. He painted some numbers on the shit house wall and everyone had to hit them with the ball and then they had to dribble round some tyres and then climb up a rope and then take penalties against titty Raymond which everybody scored even Old Ma Bowers. Then they ran round the Stadium three times and jumped over some logs. Everyone was sweating cobs at the finish and Raymond was puffing like a carthorse and looked like he were going to puke. Then they went home on their bikes.

Everybody was dead excited on the day of the Big Match and some turned up like Jim Heals and Roy's dad and Joyce Booth and Audrey and Mrs Glew etc. Kennys dad had a referee shirt and a whistle. Old Ma Bowers and

Paul and Angela had green and white scarfs. They had made Brent a sparrow hawk mascot costume with a paper mashy beak and Angelas nans feather hat. Brent went round pecking people. Old Ma Bowers had a big flask of Camp coffee for half time. Mr Nolans Juniors arrived on bikes and some of them in Mr Nolan's Morris Minor. They were very small and only about eleven but they were dirty little buggers. Our Team was R. Kirk between the sticks. R. Booth and G. Robinson as full backs. B. Robinson, J. Took, C. Tonkinson and K. Blanchard (capt) were forwards. Our loyal supporters who supported the Sparrow hawks through thick and thin were looking forward to a successful first season in the newly formed Axholme League. By half time we were 5-0 up with goals from John Took, Brian Robinson, Kenny and two from Cyril. One with his head. Mr Nolan complained that our team were too big but his team were kicking everybody and then falling over. Kenny's dad had to blow his whistle loads.

Some people had oranges. Or coffee. In the second half the Sparrow hawks are all over Nolans Juniors and then one of them kicked Roy Booth on the shins which was bleeding as Roy hadn't got any shins pads. Then the little bugger did it again and pushed past Roy and tapped the ball into the net past fat Raymond who was picking his nose. Everyone shouted save it Raymond but he didn't. So Roy was now hobbling and bleeding. The next time the Nolans kid got the ball John Took elbowed him in the face and he started crying and Kennys dad Keith sent

John Took off and Old Ma Bowers and Paul and Angela etc booed Kennys dad like mad. So we were down to six men. So then the lads pulled their fingers out and chalked up an impressive victory 17-1 and nearly everybody scored except fat Raymond. At the end Mr Nolan said it was unfair and Angela Whiteley told him to Queen's word off. It was a well deserved two points for the mighty Sparrow hawks. Next day Nolan called off the away match which tells you what a chicken he was and was also a victory for the mighty Sparrow hawks.

By now the Rovers had lost to Southend and Bury and Mansfield again and Chesterfield and Newport County and Halifax and were bottom of Div Three played 19 won 5 drawn 1 lost 13 points 11. But they beat the plucky amateurs of Consett from the Northern League 5-0 with two from Flash Mooney in the cup first round. This gave the loyal band of Rovers supporters hope for a triumphant cup run.

The next home game at the Kenny Blanchard Stadium was Westgate Wednesday against Epworth lads. It had been raining for days and the pitch was muddy and not many turned up except for the teams and Old Ma Bowers and Paul and Angela and Kennys dad who was ref. Brent didn't want to be a Sparrow hawk anymore so he stayed at home. It was a tough game and Roy and Ginger had their work cut out at the back. Epworth had a big lad up front called Malcolm Bates who scored first and then Cyril scored for us and it was 1-1 at half time. In the second half

John Took got another one kicking from miles out like Bobby Charlton and then Malcolm Bates was heading for goal so Ginger tripped him up and the ref said it was a foul when it was a legitimate tackle and so it was a penalty. And Malcolm was taking the spot kick against fat Raymond. And he saved it. He was a jammy bugger. When Malcolm shot Raymond closed his eyes and dived but slipped on the mud and ended up falling backwards and Malcolms shot hit him in the face and Roy cleared the ball upfield. Everybody cheered and the Sparrow hawks ran out worthy 2-1 winners. The away game was at the Epworth Show ground which was a proper pitch after it had been reseeded after the wrestling with proper goals etc and everything was much bigger. Epworth were a lot stronger as they were used to the big pitch. Jim Heals brought Old Ma Bowers and Paul in the wheelchair. Although our boys played well and had several chances luck was not with them. Kenny missed a sitter but their Malcolm Bates got two so we lost 2-0. Everyone was gutted but we had won 2 drawn 0 lost 1 points 4 so we had won the league as there weren't anymore fixtures so we had fish and chips from the chip shop at Grey Green when we got back home. So it was a triumphant first season for the mighty Sparrow hawks of Westgate Wednesday. Then it was the Cup Final.

The FA Cup Final was against West Butterwick because Jim Heals got the landlord of the Gun and Duck to get up a team of local lads. Old Ma Bowers was going to make the FA cup out of cardboard and silver paper but fat Raymond got one of Howard Kirks cups for clay pigeon shooting so we used that and we would win it any road. There hadn't been any rounds just the Final. The home leg was on the Friday and the away game on the Saturday. They came in the landlords van and had proper kit in Rovers colours. Their captain was called Barry Endicott. Brian Robinson called him Cockend and his dad was the landlord. Loads turned up with green scarfs and sang Abide with Me but nobody knew it except for the Methodists. Wednesday won 3-1 with goals from John Took, Kenny and Cyril Tonkinson. Their goal was when Cockend bungled fat Raymond into the back of the net like Nat Lofthouse had done against Harry Gregg last season. This season the Busby Babes had been knocked out in the third round by the Canarys of Div Three Norwich City 3-0 with two goals from Terry Bly. It was the footballing shock of the century. Rovers were knocked out by Bristol City. Kenny was going to smack Cockend but his dad told him off.

We had won and paraded the cup round the field as West Butterwick limped home to West Butterwick. Crestfallen. Everybody shouted up the Sparrow hawks. It was in the bag for tomorrow.

So Freddie Swash was going to take everybody to West Butterwick in Howard Kirks old RAF ambulance but Howard Kirk made him run a lorry load of seed potatoes over to Driffield at the last minute and Jim Heals van was full up with Old Ma Bowers and Paul and the wheelchair and the FA Cup and Angela. So everybody had to go on the bikes in their kit with their boots tied round their necks including fat Raymond and it was well over five mile. We only got there just before kick off. We were fagged out and Raymond was miles behind and had a stitch and lay on the grass and moaned. The pitch was next to the pub and on a slope. Cockends dad the landlord was referee and Kenny won the toss and said we would play down the slope but it did no good. When we kicked off they were all over us and Raymond was spastic. They were 3–0 up after 20 minutes and then all the blokes came out of the pub and cheered Cockends team and booed and laughed at Raymond and shouted lardarse greaseball etc. At half time they were 7-0 up. Old Ma Bowers put Roy Booth in goal and Raymond just waddled about looking like he was going to cry. They were now playing down the slope and threw everything they had at us but Roy was great and made hundreds of great saves diving all over the place and punching over the bar etc. They only got another two so won 10-3 on aggregate over the two legs. It was a sad disappointment for the mighty Sparrow hawks.

Kenny Blanchard presented Cockend with the Clay Pigeon FA Cup and they all had a party in the Gun and Duck.

We biked back the five miles home to Belton in our mucky kits. We left lardarse Raymond far behind. Old Ma Bowers reckoned they had been cheating by splitting their muscles. She had been told this was what Peter Swan from Armthorpe who played for Sheffield Wednesday had done. This was where you rubbed your leg muscles in a special way and they split in two so you could run twice as fast. It was illegal in the professional game. Bri Robinson got Angela to rub his legs for ages but it didn't do owt. Then Peter Swan got put in prison for taking bribes

The next Rovers home game we went to was Accrington Stanley. We had just lost 5-1 away to Halifax. We were third from bottom in the league played 41 won 13 drawn 3 lost 25 points 29 and we had to win all our remaining matches to stand a chance of avoiding relegation to the newly created Fourth Division. Rovers won 3-1 with two from Johnnie Meredith and one from new signing Irishman Frankie Callan so we were well on our way. We didn't see Greaseball Raymond. Then we lost away 3-0 at Bradford City. We were doing alright in the first half then Willy Nimmo clashed heads with their Scottish centre forward John McCole and had to go off for stitches and Big Ron had to take over in goal. Then Johnny Meredith was injured and was a passenger for the rest of the game. So we had to beat Wrexham at home to stay up but it was a 1-1 draw and Rovers were down to the newly created Div 4 from Div 2 in two seasons. It was a disaster. We all went to the last home game of the season with Hull City who had to win to be certain of promotion to Div 2. Belle Vue was nearly empty but we all cheered and rattled extra loud. The Hull supporters were football hooligans and all drunk and threw things on the pitch and swore a lot and we lost 2-0. They should never have sold Harry Gregg. After the game Charlie Williams, Tommy Cavanagh, Frankie Callan, Flash Mooney, Len Graham and even reserve keeper Billy Brough put in for transfers. They didn't want to play Fourth Division football.

But the Mighty Sparrow Hawks had won the league and were runners up in the FA Cup after only one season at the Kenny Blanchard Little Turbary Stadium.

When Howard Kirk found out that Raymond had robbed his Clay Pigeon Shooting cup and given it away he went mad. He drove over to the Gun and Duck in the bronze jag and demanded it back off of Cockend's dad. Then he beat fat Raymond with his shooting stick which had a folding seat and a metal point that he used when he went to the horse racing. Raymond was covered in bruises and couldn't go to school for days as the teachers might see them in PE. After a few days they bought him a budgie.

Be Bop A Lula

Ron Tex Robinson had not gone to Donny prison for for six months for saying the Queen's word. He had gone to prison for six months because he had found some lead on the Methodist Chapel roof that was falling off and sold it to a scrap man in Askern. Everyone knew Freddie Swash had ratted on him to the bobbies who were looking for it. Ron Tex said the Queen's word a lot. Every day.

Ron Robinson was called Ron Robinson but changed it because of Tex Ritter who was a singing cowboy. Also Ron was sort of a Teddy boy and he had been in the Navy. Ron Tex Robinson had loads of records and a wind up gramophone and an electric Dansette Bermuda record player that took eight records at once. He also sold records and second hand agricultural equipment and electrical goods etc on Donny market and other places. He got the records off jukeboxes when they were out of date and some off of sambos off of the boats in Hull. He had a lorry which was a Bedford O type flatbed. So he went round with the lorry finding things to sell and helping people shift stuff like sacks of potatoes and old tyres and roofing supplies etc that they didn't want even when he was on probation. He also had a television which everybody went to watch for the Cup Final and other things like the Army Game and Robin Hood and Ivanhoe who was a knight in armour who lived in Conisbrough Castle which is near Sprotbrough which is where Douglas Bader lives and near the farm Howard Kirk bought which Freddie Swash was going to live in but his mam didn't want to move because she wouldn't know anybody. Also Quatermass and the Pit which was dead scary about a rocket from Mars. Everybody liked the Army Game with Bootsie excused boots and Private Popeye Popplewell who said I only arsked and sang a song about how you need feet to walk to Scunthorpe for to dance the hoochy coo. Mrs Robinson was called Ada and they had Brian, Ginger Gordon and Brent. Then she was going to have another baby and Ron Tex wanted a girl called Amber Jane so they had a party in their yard.

Robinson's yard was made out of gravel with some bits of scabby grass and some petrol barrels and some stuff Ron Tex was going to sell under a tarpaulin and there was a concrete washing line. They had some cats as well.

Everybody from our end was invited. They got loads of beer from Uncle Walter at The Wheatsheaf who came himself later with some more beer and some whisky and gin. They had put the table outside and there were loads of sandwiches of potted meat and egg and some sausages and crisps etc. The Dansette Bermuda was rigged up outside and there were coloured light bulbs like at Christmas or Belton Fair which was soon. Or like the illuminations at Hexthorpe flats.

Everybody liked Ron Tex's records which were Great Balls of Fire by Jerry Lee Lewis and Rave On by Buddy Holly and the Crickets and Be Bop A Lula by Gene Vincent and Bird Dog by the Everly Brothers and I Got Stung by Elvis the King and Tallahassee Lassie by Freddy Cannon. Also She wears Red Feathers and a hula hula skirt by Guy Mitchell and Does your chewing gum lose its flavour on the bedpost overnight by Lonnie Donegan who had been on at Donny Gaumont last year. They played musical chairs and let Brent win. Then they had a treasure hunt all up the street and the treasure was a bag of chocolate money from Christmas and Kenny Blanchard found it up the polio drainpipe.

Roy Booth found an old box and put it on his head and chased everybody around saying I am Mr Box and Gordon went round as Lady Docker.

Then they had a Talent contest like Opportunity Knocks with Hughie Green and everyone had to do a turn but not everybody did as some were getting drunk.

Uncle Walter made a sausage dog out of a balloon. He wasn't anybody's Uncle Walter. He was one of Howard Kirks brothers that he didn't speak to. So he was really fat Raymond and Gillians uncle who weren't even there. Brian and Kenny sang Travelling Light by Cliff Richard. Brent did a funny Sparrow hawk dance. Old Ma Bowers and Ada Robinson and Mrs Glew were the Beverley sisters. Angela Whiteley said a poem about there was an old woman from Ealing who did a big shit on the ceiling and when she was done she wiped her fat bum on a potato peeling. She won some more chocolate money. Then Ron Tex did Mule Train with hitting himself with a tin tray like the man on Opportunity Knocks did. Then John Took knocked over the table because he had been drinking some beer and some gin and his dad had to take him home.

Then there was more dancing and Ron Tex and Ada showed everybody how to do the jive and everybody did it even Paul Bowers on his leg irons. The record was Along Came Jones by the Coasters. When it got late Ron Tex got sad and told everybody about how he wanted a girl baby called Amber Jane and how he loved Ada etc and how he was going to fix Freddie Swash. Kenny's dad Keith said leave it alone and then Jim Heals said it might not have been Freddie who dobbed him in it anyway. So Ron Tex said they could all Queen's word off so everybody went home. But some men stayed and played three card brag for money.

What happened next about Freddie Swash was Belton

Fair in the village. This was a fair nothing like as big as the St Ledger Fair in Donny or even Epworth Fair in the Show ground or Wonderland at Cleethorpes. It was neither nowt nor summat. It was on the field at Grey Green over the road from the Sir Solomon Arms in the same field as the other Rookery which was not the one where John Took puked up the bubbed rooks eggs. There was a big Fountains Fairground Amusements Steam Engine like for the threshing machine and an electric generator that hummed like thousands of wasps and there was always one big ride like a Waltzer or a Speedway or Gallopers and there was always weedy dodgems. This year there was a Caterpillar which was like a ret fast Speedway and then there was an air raid siren and then a tarpaulin sheet came over and everything went dark and the lasses all screamed and some people did other things in the dark. From outside it was reckoned to look like a caterpillar. Paul Bowers said it was more like a cocoon. Or a chrysalis. Inside it were like a smelly tent. There was a Coconut Shy and a rifle range where if you hit the bullseye a skeleton jumped up and Flying Saucers and Swingboats etc. There was a Hoopla that nobody ever won and a hook a duck where you could win a goldfish in a plastic bag. And a gypo fortune teller Rose Lee and hot dogs etc and they played Buddy Holly records dead loud. Also there were always fights. One year the Beltoft gang had a scrap with the youths from the fair over some lasses and the special constables had to come over from Crowle to sort them out.

The night we all went was the Saturday night and it was packed and everybody got popcorn and monkey nuts. Everybody went on loads of things and bashed into each other on the weedy dodgems even Old Ma Bowers and Paul who smashed loads of people. We went on the Flying Saucers and the Caterpillar. Roy Booth and Kenny nearly won a coconut which was glued on. Bri Robinson won a goldfish in a plastic bag and gave it to Angela and they went on the Caterpillar again. Gypo Rose Lee told Old Ma Bowers that she would win the pools. Ron Tex won a plaster woman with a dog for Ada on the shooting and Ginger Gordon won a paper snake on a stick on the darts that he gave to Brent who had got a toffee apple stuck in his hair. And Candy floss. Then we all went on the dodgems again and ganged up on John Took. Then the Solly Arms chucked out and all the men from the pub came to the Fair. One of them was Freddie Swash who went up to Ron Tex and grabbed hold of his jacket.

Everyone thought there would be a fight. Angela started to cry. Freddie Swash said Ron Tex should stop putting it around that he grassed on him about the lead because he never knew nowt about the lead and he hated the bloody Wesleyans and had only heard about it off Mrs Glew who was a Wesleyan and told him she had seen Ron loading the lead onto his Bedford O type flatbed when she was feeding the cats and rung the police and told them. Ron Tex said Freddie was a lying Queen's word liar but Old Ma Bowers said she would get to the bottom of it from

Mrs Glew but she didn't and Jim Heals said everybody just calm down and so there weren't a fight but Ron Tex told Freddie Swash that he had best watch his sen or he would tell the coppers that he was a bloody shirt lifter. Even though nobody had told him owt. Then everyone had some chips.

Next morning was Sunday morning and Angela took Brent to Sunday school at the Methodist Chapel. The Fair was packing up. They went to The Wheatsheaf to see Uncle Walter cos Brent wanted to see his balloon sausage dog. The pub was locked up so they went to look in the barn. Uncle Walter was hanging from a rope. Later everyone said it was because he had run out of money. He asked his brother Howard Kirk to lend him some but Howard Kirk wouldn't give him owt.

Fat Raymond's Budgie

Fat Raymond got his budgie after Howard Kirk had beaten him black and blue with his shooting stick when Raymond robbed his Clay Pigeon Trophy for the FA Cup and gave it away to Cockend in West Butterwick. They got it from the jockey Stan Clayton's mam who bred fancy budgies. It was the runt of the litter. Like Raymond. Raymond called it Georgie and it was yellow and sick and couldn't fly and its legs were spastic like Paul Bowers. Raymond thought Georgie loved him because he didn't fly away. He thought he had special powers over budgies. Raymond kept Georgie in his pocket and took it everywhere and got him to eat birdseed out of his mouth. At night the budgie slept in bed with him. Raymond tried to teach it tricks like ringing a bell or pushing a ball or saying Georgie but it didn't. Also he tried to teach it to fly by pulling out its wings and blowing on his feathers and throwing it up in the air but the dog nearly got it. Gillian hated the budgie and so did Olive Oil. They hoped the dog would get it. Raymond took it to school to show everybody his power over budgies.

Every morning Olive Oil took fat Raymond and Gillian to their posh schools in Donny in her blue Austin A30. It was fifteen mile and you had to go over the old aerodrome at Sandtoft. You had to drive around the old runways and past the old conning tower and big rusty hangers which were just skeletons as Ron Tex and others like the squatters had taken all the corrugated iron away. There were hundreds of peewits. The squatters lived in the squatters camp which was some huts and cook house etc left behind from when it was the RAF before it was the Itie prisoners. The squatters were families and their kids whose houses had been bombed by Hitler from Hull and Sheffield and had nowt and no houses and they had just moved in. They kept to their sens and had water and electric and everything and it never cost them owt. Except then it went all round the village that they were stealing pet dogs and cats and were eating them and Old Ma Bowers and others had seen it with their own two eyes. So Howard Kirk in his bronze jag and some of the farmers and masons and some from the village like Ron Tex and John Took's dad went over there one night with shotguns and moved them on. Then the RAF sold the sheds.

Every day on the way to school Olive Oil told Raymond she wished he had never been born and that he was so fat and ugly he would never get a wife and she would be stuck with him forever and then she hit him still driving and said she would swing for him. Gillian just sat there and read her Bunty ballerina comic. Fat Raymond was so scared that Olive Oil would kill him in the night that he slept with a sheath knife under his pillow. When he got to school with Georgie the budgie they had found out about the sixteen footballs. In the Hotspur comic you could collect cards of world footballers and there was a competition to pick the best world team. It was a game of skill and you had to fill in a coupon with all the names and it said the prizes were sixteen footballs. Fishy Addock and Raymond got all the cards and picked a world best eleven out of Puskas and Jules Fontaine and Didi and VaVa and Pele and Garrincha and Raymond Kopa and Alfredo di Stefano and Billy Wright and John Charles and Danny Blanchflower and Lev Yashin and Helmut Rahn and Nils Liedholm and Francisco Gento and Ladislav Novak and Ivan Kolev and Bobby Charlton and Bengt Gustavsson and Wilbur Cush and Harry Gregg etc. So they picked the best team and fat Raymond sent in the coupon and told all the rich kids at the posh Mount school who didn't like him that if he won the sixteen footballs they could all have one. But he never sent it in. But then Fishy and the other lads asked him if he had heard owt and Raymond told him they had won and he was just waiting for the sixteen footballs to arrive in the post and they could all have one. He was such a ruddy liar and he had lied about being in his school team cos he wasn't. Nowhere near. Everybody said how clever Raymond and Fishy were at picking the best world football team in the Hotspur including the teachers.

But then on the day that he took Georgie to school the Hotspur came out with the list of the sixteen winners who had won the sixteen footballs and none of them were fat Raymond. So they gave him a chinese burn and said they were going to beat him up in break so he hid in the toilets with the budgie. Then the fog came down.

The fog was worse than fog it was smog. It was yellow and stinky and all the smoke and chemicals from the blast furnaces in Scunny and Sheffield got caught up in it and you couldn't see your hand in front of your face. Howard Kirk had to pick Gillian and Raymond up from school as Olive Oil wouldn't drive in the fog because once she had been driving over the aerodrome it came down and she got lost and stopped the car and when it cleared after hours she had drove inside the skeleton of one of the rusty hangers and she could have been killed. So Howard Kirk picked up Gillian and Raymond in the bronze jag and Raymond and his budgie sat in the front and Gillian who was the apple of his eye sat in the back and nobody said owt as Howard Kirk had to concentrate on his driving. When you got to the Green Tree pub outside Hatfield you had to go down Hatfield Straight which was a straight road six miles long with a dyke on both sides and just fields until Sandtoft. Howard Kirk told Raymond to light his cigar. In the dashboard of the Mark 7 Jaguar there was a special electric cigar lighter that you pushed in and when it came out it was red hot and you could light your cigar with it. Raymond pushed it in but it shot right out and burnt Howard Kirk on his trousers. Howard Kirk stopped the car and belted Raymond and kicked him out of the car in the middle of nowhere. Then he drove off. Then he threw out the budgie. Raymond looked for Georgie but couldn't find it. It was lost. Maybe in the Dyke. A rat probably got it. Raymond just walked on crying in the fog and saw a ghost. Then after hours he saw some lights coming. It was Freddie Swash in his Cortina who Howard Kirk had sent to pick him up.

Old Ma Bowers found out all this off Jim Heals who heard it off Freddie Swash and everyone thought it was shit what Howard Kirk did throwing fat Raymond and the budgie out of the car but not much as Raymond had told them they were also going to get the sixteen footballs. Old Ma Bowers said fat Raymond was a bloody liar and deserved it but then she could talk.

When the fog had gone Howard Kirks daughter Fran came from Kettering in their Humber Super Snipe which was a fast luxury car completely equipped but not too costly. Frans mam was the second Mrs Kirk who had done the special rabbits with Olive Oil. Fran was a sister nurse in the hospital in Kettering and married a doctor called Johnny who was South African but not a darkie. Johnny liked to drive fast. They had two kids called Annette and Christopher who were also snobs. Olive Oil didn't like Fran because she was bossy and bossed everybody around even Howard Kirk as she was the apple of his eye before Gillian was apple of his eye except she never got a pony. They also brought their own food like nuts and special porridge and Dettol soap because of the countryside germs and they were cranks. They had come to sort out fat Raymond. Fran said they should put Raymond in a loony bin and had brought some papers to sign and Olive Oil signed them. Like father like son. Fat Raymond and Annette and Christopher went for a walk and Annette showed them her bottom in the railway carriage.

Dr Johnny liked guns because he was from South Africa so next day they all went Clay Pigeon shooting and Raymond blew Howard Kirks head off with his 12 bore. It was an accident.

That'll Be the Day

This is what it said in the Epworth Bells.

Few deaths in the Isle in recent years have come with so sudden a shock, for Mr Howard Kirk was one of the best known men in the area, nor was knowledge of him confined merely to the Isle. He was a one-time blacksmith's boy who after becoming a blacksmith himself began farming and went into the produce trade, building up one of the biggest merchant businesses in the district.

It is not always that great popularity goes with wellknownness, but in Howard Kirk's case it did, and many are the tributes which have been paid as news of his death passed though the Isle of his tragic death in a shooting accident.

His insignia one might almost say, was his button hole and his Churchill cigar. He was hardly ever seen without one and not often without the other. Whenever there was a flower in his own garden, he himself would wear it for the day on his jacket lapel. When there were roses it was always a rose.

These two 'trade marks' were always an honest pleasure to him, not an ostentation; yet they did in a sense mark what one who knew him closely has described as the flamboyant side to his unassuming disposition.

For instance he made donations to efforts and causes, but they were always anonymous to all except those to whom they were handed.

Old Ma Bowers said it served him right and it was God's punishment and he had always been a right mean bastard even when he had nowt and he might have given some of the money for Pauls wheelchair but it were him that put him in it to begin with. And what about Uncle Walter.

With Clay Pigeon shooting what you shoot at is a spinning target like a jukebox record made out of clay not plastic or a flying saucer. This is shot up into the air by a sort of automatic catapult machine when you pull the string. You shout pull when you are ready to shoot. It is for practice for shooting pheasants when its not in season. Howard Kirk had his own catapult machine and set it up in the pea field behind Common Farm with Freddie Swash pulling the string so Dr Johnny from South Africa could have a go. Howard Kirk had won many cups and awards for clay pigeon shooting and could shoot two at once. So Dr Johnny had a go and Fran had a go and didn't hit owt. Then Howard Kirk got ready to shoot and fat Raymond was next in line. Then Howard said pull and as he shot Raymonds gun went off as well by accident. There are three hundred and fifty lead balls in a 12 bore shotgun cartridge and they all went through Howard Kirks head which burst open and exploded. Everybody was screaming and crying and carrying on and covered in blood and bits of brain and some puked up. Fat Raymond said it was nowt to do with him as it was an accident. Dr Johnny and Fran tried to stop the bleeding but gave up and the ambulance and cop cars all came racing through the village with their bells ringing and everyone went out to see what was going off. They put the bits of Howard Kirk in a bag and took them to Scunthorpe Memorial Hospital but was too late. Then they gave everybody sleeping pills to calm them down. Old Ma Bowers told everybody about all this. She had been told by Jim Heals who had been told by Freddie Swash who had seen it all with his own two eyes. The Police were going to lock up Raymond for shooting his dad but didn't when the Chief Inspector arrived and said the safety catch was broke and said it were an accident. Not everybody believed it were an accident.

Hundreds of people turned out for the funeral. There was the whole Kirk family with Olive Oil and Gillian and

Raymond who weren't in prison cos it were an a accident and Dr Johnny and Fran and Annette and Christopher and they were all kitted out in black frocks and suits and Herbert and Harry and Arthur and George the other brothers of Howard Kirk who he never spoke to and their wives etc. And also there were all the farmers and freemasons because Howard was a high master or summat and people from the Isle of Axholme Branch of the NFU and Epworth Show and men from Selby Canning Factory and the special constables from Crowle etc.

A big black Bentley with big windows took the coffin covered in wreaths made to look like peas, washed carrots and potatoes and a big one from Fran saying Daddy round the whole village on the same course as the Barrow Race passing all five pubs and ending up at the Church. Some people had a pint in all the pubs. Everybody went outside to watch it. All the men took their hats off and everybody closed their curtains like when the king died. Everybody from our end stood on the bridge over the Dyke including Paul Bowers in his wheelchair and Old Ma Bowers, Kenny and Bri and Ginger Robinson and Brent and his mam Ada and Roy Booth and Angela all watched fat Raymond going past in the big black family car. Kenny shouted Up the Rovers to cheer him up but he still just looked miserable. When the funeral went past The Wheatsheaf some turned their backs. When the funeral went past the Sir Solomon they had the flag at half mast. Some men clapped and raised their pints. Some didn't.

At the All Saints Church at the top of the village Freddie Swash and Raymond and Barry Dodds and some farmers from the NFU potato committee carried the coffin inside with a rose on it inside past the graves of the old dead people and the second wife Grace who was Fran's mam. Then they sang Love divine all loves excelling and then the vicar said how sad it was and a horrible accident and how Howard Kirk was a great family man and farmer and Christian and gave loads of money away to poor people and had a cigar etc. He didn't say owt about Howard Kirk going mad in Lincoln or the poisoned cows on the Big Turbary or Uncle Walter. Then everybody sang Abide with me. Then Gillian Kirk who had posh speaking lessons read summat from the bible called the good samaritans but she couldn't get her words out for tears of snot running down her face. Then the choir sang Low he comes with clouds descending.

When they put him in the ground the Vicar thought Olive Oil was dead upset and fainting so he put his arm round her and said Jesus has promised that they will be united in heaven. Olive Oil said nowt but threw some muck on the coffin.

After the funeral everyone went back to the Methodist Hall where they had the Harvest Festival and the Jumble sales because there was more room and they had a bit of a do. Mrs Booth and Joyce Booth and others had made loads of tinned salmon and cucumber sandwiches and ham sandwiches and pilchards on toast and pies and

Angela Whiteley passed them round. There was loads of beer and gin as well. Ron Tex brought his gramophone and they played Howards George Formby records like with his little ukulele in his hand.

The posh people all stood down one end and the village people stood down the other end and all the farm workers stood about in their wedding suits with black arm bands smoking fags. Herbert, Harry, Arthur and George and their wives were all in different corners because they didn't speak to each other either. Old Ma Bowers said it went back a long way and was about livestock. Lots of other stuff came out about Howard Kirk. Old Ma Bowers reckoned that the loony witch in the attic down the lane to the Big Turbary was Howard Kirks first wife and she was a nag so he had got her locked up so he could marry Grace but Barry Dodds said that were a load of balls and the witch went mad because they took her baby away and Ma Bowers knew nowt.

Everyone was being dead nice to Olive Oil and Gillian and saying they were sorry about the shooting accident etc. Roy Booth and Ginger told Raymond that he could be in goal for the Sparrow hawks next season but John Took said could he ekkers like and over his dead body. Ron Tex had some gin and went up to Mrs Glew and said did she grass him up about the Methodist lead and she said she couldn't tell a lie in Gods holy chapel and it was her and Ron Tex called her a Queen's word fucking nosey bitch and Mrs Glew went home crying and carrying on and Old Ma Bowers said it served her right and she never cleaned her windows. Then Ron Tex went to Freddie Swash and shook his hand and we never told him about Freddie showing his bottom in Jim Heals van. When the posh people and the Kirks went home Ron Tex put on the Buddy Holly and everyone did some jiving and some did some snogging and stuff to celebrate the death of Howard Kirk by accident.

The first Rovers home game of our first season in the newly formed Div Four was Northampton. Our Manager Mr Jack Crayston knew that our faithful supporters would join him in expressing the hope that our stay in this division will only be a short one. It will be a hard fight, we know that, but with a fixed determination and loyalty from our players and supporters we believe that we shall succeed. In the close season we signed midfield general Albert Broadbent from Rotherham United and Tony Leighton from Leeds but failed to sign former international inside forward Jackie Sewell from Birmingham City for domestic reasons. We all went in the back of Ron Tex's lorry but it was a tight fit what with Old Ma Bowers and Paul Bowers wheelchair and loads of old stuff as Freddie Swash was now helping Ron Tex to find ploughs and old fencing etc that they didn't probably need anymore on Common Farm. We stood behind Willy Nimmos goal and rattled and cheered like mad. There weren't many there as we had already lost away to the Seasiders of Torquay United and drawn 0-0 with Millwall. Fat

Raymond weren't there as he couldn't go out anymore. It was great game and Rovers won 3-2. Lol Chappell scored with a strained leg but carried on and Jimmy Fernie got the other two. Then we beat Watford 1-0 at home and so the Mighty Rovers were riding high again. Then we lost to Barrow and Gateshead and Carlisle away and Aldershot and Darlington and Notts County and Exeter City and the Seasiders of Torquay again at home. And Walsall and Crewe and Crystal Palace away and half way through the season we were won 6 drawn 4 lost 13 points 16 and third from bottom of the newly formed Div Four. Alick Jeffrey went to Skegness Town for practice but broke his leg again and went to Australia to get better.

It turned out that Howard Kirk never made a will so Olive Oil got most of it and there was some for Fran, Gillian and Fat Raymond. But then they found out that Howard Kirk had never paid his taxes and also death duty so Olive Oil had to sell the whole lot to pay it off. In the end there wasn't that much left. Common Farm was sold to Major Stubley who already had a big house in Skellow so didn't want to live in the farm house so he made Freddie Swash farm manager and he moved in and sold the bungalow. Jim Heals helped him do up the farm cottage for his mam who were on her last legs any road. Gillian went to ballet school up in London. Stargazer was sold off to the jockey Stan Clayton who had won the Yorkshire Oaks for his sister. The masons paid for Raymond to go to a special boarding school for masons and Olive Oil opened up a pet shop in Northallerton where she came from in the first place.

There was a new bus on Saturdays that went into Scunny and back so everyone stopped going to the Rovers for a bit and went to Scunny where there was a new coffee bar called the Buccaneer which was done out like a Pirate ship. You could just have a coffee and there were parrots and cannon balls etc and some lasses. Also there was the Wimpy. Brian Robinson and Angela went to see a pop singer called Dickie Pride who shook and sang at the same time at the Pavilion Picture House. Everybody thought he were daft. Then Old Ma Bowers and Paul wanted to get the Mighty Sparrow hawks going again but it never happened. Kennys dad hated living on the Little Turbary more than Grimsby so he got his old job back on the docks and Kenny had to move back to Cleethorpes. And the Beltoft gang robbed the goalposts for Bonfire Night.

The last Rovers game of the season people went to was at home with Stockport County. Our fortunes had improved. We had a run of six games without defeat and beat Hartlepool 6-2 away (Clark 4, Leighton, Broadbent) which was one for the record books and then Crewe Alexander at home 4-0 (Fernie 2, Broadbent, Clark) so we were no longer staring reelection to Div Four in the face. Also Rovers had a warning from the FA when a bloke from Edlington punched the ref in the gob after our 1-1 draw at home to Walsall. Old Ma Bowers and Paul didn't come to Stockport and went to Scunny on the bus because Paul had to get measured for new calipers and everyone missed Kenny and Fishy didn't come without fat Raymond. Rovers won but it were nowt like the glory days of the Four Musketeers of Alick Jeffrey Harry Gregg Charlie Williams and Flash Mooney. At the end of the season we had played 46 won 16 lost 20 drawn 10 points 42 so the future once again looked bright for the mighty Donny Rovers.

The eels came back to the Drain. Roy Booth saw one from the bridge and went to get his landing net to catch it but John Took shot at it with his airgun and tried to catch it but it bit him on his face and it went septic and he had to go to Hospital for a jab or he would have gone mad. Old Ma Bowers said it served him right. Brian and Ginger Gordon and Brent got a baby sister called Amber Jane and Ron Tex had another party to wet the babys head with Buddy Holly and Little Richard etc and everybody did more jiving and it wasn't true that you went to prison if you said the Queen's word. Old Ma Bowers had made it all up.

CB *editions*

Founded in 2007, CB editions publishes chiefly short fiction and poetry, including work in translation. Books can be ordered from www.cbeditions.com.